BETTER AS FRIENDS

BOOK ONE IN THE CASSIDY AND CAHIR SERIES

JIMI GAILLARD-JEFFERSON

I'm going to be bold-
This book is for me. For surviving.

ONE

Cahir

SHE CALLED to me like a siren. No. That's not right. Zion wasn't just a siren. She was their queen. And she didn't call to me. She sang. Her songs matched the blood rushing through my veins and the pace of my lungs as they accepted and rejected air. Her songs sounded like the flow of my thoughts. Not the individual thoughts themselves, just the way my mind moved from one concept to the next.

Of course it was natural to fall in love with her. I felt understood in a way that was unfamiliar to me, in a way that made me crave her. It was why I chased her through restaurants and hotel lobbies after she left me. It was what pushed my feet to her house even though her song was gone and she had no words for me. It was why I raised her body high before bringing her to crash down around me.

Then she told me.

Abortion. An abortion. That was why she'd run? The tempo of her song changed just a bit, and I was out of step. For the first time there was the sense of effort between us.

She once felt like air and food and water and rest. Shouldn't she have known me better? Shouldn't she have known that my life was about the deal, about rising high only to see the weakness in others and sell them solutions? What would I do with a child? I didn't know what to do with all of the things I felt for her. I was supposed to add more? Welcome another? No, the abortion was the right choice. The best choice. The only choice.

I used my softest words, roughest touch. I made love, and I fucked. I gathered her close and slapped her face the way she liked. I stretched myself from one end of the earth to the other to show her that I was still hers. I was still a supplicant at her altar. Bones chilled, knees ached, mind freed. I was still hers. She was still mine. We didn't need a baby to complete us.

It became a mantra. Perhaps I could say the words so often I would no longer be able to see. The altar was broken. My queen was weak. Oh, she still stood tall but there were moments. I would speak and where there should have been her soft voice with its careful syllables and galaxies of meaning there was only silence.

I knew better than to turn to her. I knew better than to show her that I saw. I watched from the corners of my eyes as her body waved in a wind only she could feel.

I still went to her. The melody of the song changed, but it was still my song. Still my siren. And wasn't I careful? Didn't I change everything to make sure she wouldn't leave me again? Condoms hidden all over her apartment. Desire between us was sudden and insistent. I wanted to be ready. I wanted to be safe. I wanted an eternity with her.

When I was inside her, it felt like an eternity. Or maybe it was an absence. Of time. Of thought. Of awareness. There was nothing in the world but her. Even I went away.

Then I heard the sounds of her pleasure. The sounds of release and time would rush towards me. I would drop like lead back into my own body and hold still, hold onto her, for just a moment. Just a moment to find my legs again, to let her tether me back to her.

I remember I smiled that particular time. Because that time felt like what we had before the pregnancy changed us. And I knew it. I knew it! I knew if she just gave us a chance we could be what we were again. I knew that she was wrong. We didn't need a baby to complete us. We were complete. We were more than enough on our own.

She saw. She knew. She smiled the smile I remembered and it felt like my song was what it used to be. It felt like she trusted me to lead, to guide, to be her man.

I smiled when I pulled the condom off. I knotted it tight. I pulled the knot. I was a man but once I was a boy who liked things that oozed or moved in odd ways in confined spaces.

My smile fell. There was real ooze. Real-What was in my hand? I didn't understand. Why was there a mess in my hand?

I smelled it. And where there should have been the scent of Zion and latex there was the smell of us together.

No.

I remember that was the only word I could find. No. She wouldn't do that to me. She wouldn't manipulate me. She wouldn't go behind my back. She wouldn't force me into a situation I didn't want. She would take the magic that was our sex and manipulate it, make it ugly. Make it rape.

I curled back from that word. Not me. Not me. Men didn't have that happen to them. When women forced sex, forced a change in sex, it was a compliment. It was only ugly when men did it to them. That was it.

That was all.

And I was wrong. There was nothing wrong with the condom. I just wasn't careful when I took it off. I'd always been careful before. Careful meant I went back to Zion sooner. But I couldn't be careful every time. Eventually there was bound to be a mess. I would prove it.

I held the condom under the sink faucet and waited for it to fill with water like the water balloons I used to throw in the summer. I smiled while I waited. Sure that I would be proven wrong. Sure that I would stumble, laughing, from the bathroom to tell Zion about my silliness.

But the condom didn't swell. Not really. The six holes in it made it easier for water to flow out of it. I stuck my hand under that water. I turned off the sink. Put my hand under the condom again. Maybe if I held my hand there long enough the water would become something else. Or I would wake up. I was willing to give up everything I had if it could all just be a bad dream, if it could be me instead of Zion that woke up screaming.

The water stopped. I filled the condom again. Watched it empty again. Fill. Empty. Fill. Empty. I thought I was empty too. Then I thought about what my life would be like with a baby and a woman that was happy to manipulate me, discard my feelings, alter the course of my life whether I wanted her to or not and claim it was in the name of love. Whether I agreed or not.

Didn't the loss of consent make it rape?

I punched the mirror with my right fist then my left. Blood, semen, and water mixed and coagulated over my hands.

There was Zion in the doorway, mouth open and ready to admit, without sorrow, shame, or subterfuge, what she'd done.

That was always when I woke up. And like I did every time the dream woke me, I ran my hand over the scars left by the damage I'd done and the stitches Fine gave me. He was the only one that tried to put me back together. I reached across the empty space that should have held her body and realized that it was a nightmare. It was just a nightmare.

One that happened to me in reality and chased me into my sleep.

∞

Cassidy

THEY WEREN'T JUST CLOTHES. They were my chance to peek into your soul and see what you hid there, what you valued. To find the parts of your body that you hated. To find out when you had the best and worst times of your life and if you healed from them. Did you love yourself? Did you hate the world? Were you insecure? Which way did you lean politically? Were you rich? Were you poor? Could you live within your means? Were you a good liar?

It took just a glance to know if you were a follower, a leader, or trying to shrink into the background. In a matter of seconds, I knew more about you than you would willingly admit to yourself.

I wouldn't let anyone say it's just clothes.

I wouldn't let anyone say my job as a personal stylist was easy. The majority of you hated your bodies. You paid me to do more than dress you. You paid me to make you fall in love with yourself. You paid me to make you believe that your dreams could come true. Wasn't that what you thought when you slipped on the outfit that made you feel like you could handle your day and it's challenges, that you could get that certain someone's attention, that you could hang with the cool kids?

Did you think it was easy to find the lovable parts of you before you did?

Exhausting. All exhausting. It was what waited at the core of the exhaustion that brought me back to the job over and over again. At the core was exhilaration. I never failed. I struck rock and flint and saw a spark come into your eyes that I knew would become a blaze. I knew I had you. You were my addict.

I was tired when Cahir came into Beyond to be styled. I knew who he was. I heard snatches of whispers about him and Zion. Never the whole story. I just knew Zion was gone. It would have been nice to get a happy person for once. To be able to step over the broken birds and get someone whole.

I couldn't say no to Delia though. Not when she gave me everything I ever wanted in a job. Not when she respected me and my ideas.

I sighed and pulled out an empty rack. Tom Ford. Versace. Zegna. Gucci. Calvin Klein. A few bespoke Seville pieces. Not that the options mattered. He would wear what I gave him.

"Excuse me? I'm here to see Delia?"

Something in me jumped. That part of me that could get hot, soft, liquid. The part of me that moaned and panted and begged and screamed and scratched and clawed. I missed that part of me. She hid from me after Kevin. I didn't try to draw her out or coax her back into her place. I thought she deserved that, deserved the break.

I stepped from behind the rack and blinked. I called

myself a liar. I said I knew Cahir. I was so wrong. I knew of him. I knew his name and his reputation for building tech companies whose sole purpose was to be sold for billions to specific and exacting buyers. I knew his net worth.

I didn't know he was over six feet and all shoulders and broad arms. I didn't know his skin was a perfect meeting of untreated maple and delicate spring roses. I didn't know his lips were full and looked as ready to laugh as they were to sin. I didn't know his eyes were the color of the earth I turned over in the summer with my grandmother and filled with seeds. And his hands...

The earth wasn't the only thing that could be filled with seed and-

I couldn't help it. I burst into laughter at myself. Bless his heart, he only slid his hands into the pockets of his pants. He only showed me he had the thighs to match the arms and a crisp white shirt to pull tight over a chest I could bite.

"Delia?"

"Sorry." I snorted. "I'm not. The thing that just ran through my head was ridiculous."

He grinned. No, it was a ghost of a grin that made me want to see the real thing. "What was it?"

"I can't tell you. It was about you, and it was wildly inappropriate." I went to him, hand outstretched. "I'm Cassidy. You're seeing me. Not Delia."

"Oh." The grin fell from his face and made my joy feel inappropriate.

There was no fun anymore. It was a shame to lose it. When I looked at him and saw what I saw there was something else. I saw a man that was attracted to the woman in front of him. And I was pleased. Not because a man's attention and attraction were rare. I was five ten with a willowy body that made people think I was a model not a stylist. I wore my red-brown curls in an Afro so big and wild it felt like my own personal halo. No. It wasn't seeing his attraction. It was seeing my own. The spark. It was knowing that I was ready to have fun in spite of myself. In spite of what Kevin did to me.

But there was his sorrow. And more. There was something else that filled the space between us that had nothing to do with Delia and everything to do with the woman who used to occupy the office next to her: Zion.

Broken birds.

And wasn't I broken myself after Kevin?

I did what my grandmother taught me. I let all the emotions mix with my breath. The disappointment, the attraction, the lust, the hope that I was ready to move forward and found...something. I let it all mix together, and then I opened my mouth and released it.

A second to close my eyes and thank each of the emotions for choosing me, for reminding me of the weight and beauty of being human. I thanked the universe for giving me something nice to look at and dress. The clothes would hang well on him. They would be worn by him. So often, despite everything I did, it was the other way around. Gratitude. It swelled in my belly and made me feel warm.

"Let's get started," I said. "Tell me what you want to feel like after you get dressed."

TWO

Cassidy

I MET Junie the day after I started at Beyond. She strode into Delia's loft office and sat down on the couch next to me. Her braids were highlighter yellow, and the gum she popped and blew into large bubbles smelled like watermelon.

"I'm Junie. I was going to get into your business yesterday, but O'Shea wouldn't let me. Something about pretending to be civilized until your employment paperwork was filed."

I laughed. Looked her over. Pretty. Long features that would have been horsey on anyone else but were elegant and strong on her. Chiseled. Dark skin. Bamboo hoop earrings. "What you have is a gift."

"Which one are you talking about? My ability to spot a trash nigga or fight?"

I laughed again. Really laughed. No one made me really laugh but my grandmother. "Urban. Not everyone can make urban look so classy."

"Class is a myth. Looking classy isn't a skill." She waved a hand and popped her gum. Twice. "Any woman that knows she's fine and walks with a purpose can make a tattered bathrobe look like magic. Now. Tell me all your business."

I did. I told her everything. More than I'd ever told a person about myself so fast. But there was something about Junie that reminded me of the hottest summer days I could remember. The way I tried to hold the heat close to me, to spend every second in it that I could. Junie, like a summer day, felt like she had the power to make me forget the worst of it, to forget winter was coming.

I brought her coffee in the morning, and she brought me the paper, she made sense of the financial section and told me where to invest. I gave her clothes and accessories and helped her dye the hair she braided into her own. And every day after work, every day, we went out for drinks.

Junie left work when she felt like it. "Nadia tells me what to do. But she sure as shit ain't ever going to tell me what to do. Tuh." She would text me an address, and I met her there. We had two drinks. Only two. Junie said she always forgot who she was when she was drunk, and that wasn't safe for anyone. And alcohol made me bloated for days. I couldn't afford that. My clothes were specifically tailored to fit me at a specific size.

I met her at a place we went to before. One of those places with black penny tiles on the floor and gold sconces on the wall. Marble bar and a man with delicious muscles shucking oysters behind a high glass wall. Booths too large for anything less than eight people held two people who probably did things to each other under the table no one wanted to know about.

We both admitted the drinks weren't great but the

people watching was phenomenal. I always picked up a few clients when we visited. Junie picked up rich men that always looked like they couldn't quite believe she deigned to speak to them. I once watched a man rub his hands with glee after she dismissed him.

"You didn't tell me Cahir was fine." My purse was heavy when it hit the solid marble of the bar.

"He was fucking a New Money Girl. What the fuck else was he going to be?" Junie took a sip of her drink and flipped teal braids over her shoulder.

"Is Guy fine?" I settled into my barstool and smiled at the bartender.

"When he looks at O'Shea," Junie said.

"Yeah." I nodded my head. "That's true. Oh, thank you."

I took a sip of the ice cold Cosmo and sighed.

"That bad?" Junie popped her gum.

"How do you chew gum and drink things? My gum always gets hard."

"Strong jaw." Junie's grin was sly.

My laughter boomed. "Bitch."

"So Cahir, huh?"

"That's a good looking man."

"Better looking than Kevin?"

I smirked.

"You ain't never met a more off-limits man in your life."

"What? Why?"

"Zion's ex? Come on, Cass. I don't have to explain this to you."

"Ex. That's the word I want us to focus on." I didn't know what I was doing. I didn't understand the words that came out of my own mouth. I didn't want Cahir. I just liked looking at him.

"That one didn't end pretty. Everyone's still got scars from that one. Including me. And I didn't like the bitch."

"What?" I set my drink down on the bar.

Everyone tiptoed around Zion's office, looked at it without seeing it. Her name was said in whispers. It wasn't said around O'Shea at all. She was a wound that festered and oozed on what would have otherwise been a pristine place.

"She never had the time for me. Couldn't say hi when she walked in the door. Looked at me the way some black girls look at each other. You know what I mean. Looked at me like I should leave that 'hood' shit outside and speak 'proper' English. Like my kind of black wasn't the kind she could be around."

"Really?"

"But it don't matter how I felt about her. That was their sister. And they go to the wall, shit, through the wall for each other. Leave that man alone."

"Whatever."

Not like I wanted him anyways.

∞

Cassidy

I ONLY ATTENDED the event because I had a dress for it. A dress that hung in my closet and called to me, called for me, begged to be worn, to be seen. I obeyed the call and was glad I did. It clung to my body the way rain clung to roofs and asphalt. I was brighter in it. New in it. More because of it. I tamed my curls just a bit. I twisted them the way my grandmother used to before she let me go play in the thunderstorms. And then I took those twists

out and loved that my hair looked like a cloud. I liked
feeling close to heaven. Like I was my own kind of
heaven.

My heels were high, but I liked towering over people,
over men. I liked the way they had to crane their heads back
to see me. I liked looking down on them and seeing all the
ways I could dress them better. I liked that they believed
me, and soon I didn't have a business card on me. God, it
felt good to be good.

I drank champagne and danced with some of the girls I
styled. The ones that danced in my office and let me photo-
graph them. The ones that knew it was me that got them the
husbands, the jobs, the spread in the style or lifestyle
sections of the paper or their favorite magazines. They kept
me close during that party. Too close. Their sweat, as they
moved wild and fast on the dance floor, streaked on my
arms, and I had to go. Did they wash? Any part of their
body? Could I trust them or did I just like the clothes they
wore?

I burst off the dance floor and into a dark hallway.
Thank God for the cool that lived in dark hallways. I
snagged another glass of champagne from a waiter that
walked past and felt the soft touch of relief.

"You're always so beautiful."

"Yes. I am." I didn't turn to the deep baritone that
drifted down the hall to me. I didn't have to. I knew it the
way I knew myself. I heard it when it wasn't near. I always
heard him. I felt him.

"I miss you."

"And your wife misses you, Kevin." I was proud that
there was no bitterness. Proud that my rituals for release, for
tranquility and acceptance, worked. I had never done them
without my grandmother before.

"Don't bring her into this, C. She's not a part of this. She's never been a part of who we are. What we've done."

What we'd done. Oh. The things we'd done. The places we did it. I could smell him when I knew he wasn't around. It always knocked me on my ass and made me want to open my mouth and beg him for more even though I knew he wouldn't hear.

But she was there. Always there. The stain on the sheets that I couldn't see. The film on my skin when it wasn't touching his. The moan that sounded like I'd wrenched it from his body instead of welcoming it gently. The moment when he looked away and I didn't know where he'd gone and instinctually knew not to probe.

"Go back to the party, Kevin. Go back to your wife. Tonight, before you go to bed, kiss your children." And, oh, that hurt. He never told me there were children. I saw them. In my dreams, I saw them. Beautiful babies with his kinky hair and dimpled smile. The boy would be tall like him. The girl was already as stubborn.

I turned to him and saw him stagger back. I was ashamed for a second. I went against what my grandmother taught me: I enjoyed another's pain. I fed on his shock and was full like a glutton with room for a bit more. I took a step.

"Go home and read the things your wife left for you on her desk." I visited his wife's dreams once. And I was sad for her, for how much she yearned for him and was afraid for him, for his business. "You have time to stop it."

His fear and surprise tasted better than his dick ever had. "Cass-"

I smiled. I had time to eat him before I went back to the party. It wouldn't make the hurt any less but, Jesus, it would be fun.

"Cassidy."

Again the part of me that used to reach out like a greedy child for Kevin went warm. "Cahir."

Tom Ford was perfection on him. "There you are. I saw you leave the dance floor but Angelo had something to tell me. He said it was important, but you know how asinine he is."

Cahir's arm snaked around me. Loose, but familiar. Sure, but questioning. He was the only man besides Kevin I couldn't look down on that night.

I laughed. I didn't know who Angelo was. I didn't have to. I loved games. "I don't know if he'd be okay with you calling him that."

"Truth is the truth." Cahir shrugged. "You done with this?"

"Yes." I couldn't do anything that would top the look Cahir's presence put on Kevin's face.

"Good." His arm was gone, and then he was. Just a few steps down the hall. He stopped. Turned to me. Held out his hand. "You coming?"

"Yes."

THREE

Cassidy

HE COULD DANCE. I didn't expect that and felt a little shame. I fought so hard against the stereotypes placed on Black women and put one right on that Asian man.

Shit.

He moved like the shadows thrown by the moon. Something a little seductive and dangerous in the way he didn't forget he had hips and a loose waist when he slid through space with me. And he smiled. Bright smile through it all. Danced and danced and danced with me. He laughed at me when I fanned my face, panted, and tried to get off that floor. Grabbed my hand and held onto it. Held onto me. And wasn't that a different kind of comfortable and cozy? I laughed and thought it sounded new. I liked that.

I liked what my night became. I liked how much my feet hurt and pulsed against the sides of my shoes. I liked the feel of a few curls plastered to the back of my neck. I liked the beads of sweat that grew in the land between my edges and my forehead. I liked the burn of my thighs. The soreness in my ass from bouncing just a bit too hard.

I stayed on the dance floor with him.

∞

Cassidy

DID he know what we were laughing about? We ran together out of that charity event, my hand held firmly in his, into brisk night air that moved with sharp purpose over our skin. That air raised goosebumps and the awareness that what we had was one of those perfect nights. One of those magic nights that could turn the mundane into miracles.

Ah.

Down the steps. I expected to lose a shoe. Only one. It was the kind of thing that happened on nights like those. But I didn't lose my shoe. I thought I lost my mind. I got into his car. A strange man's car. I let him drive, and I laughed when I looked at him the way he laughed when he looked at me. I looked out the window at the moon. It wasn't full. I had no one but myself to blame my behavior on.

He took us to the obnoxious Italian restaurant. The one that played Rat Pack songs loud from hidden speakers and had lights strung across trees that had carried enough burden in their lives and deserved to be free.

I almost stopped laughing.

But he tugged me past that place and towards the unmarked door a little further back. Back in the shadows, the dark, the corner. Oh. How good and right. I laughed into the dark he pulled me into. Laughed into velvet curtains and thick, thick hardwood floors. Past the hostess who dropped the tired from her face and smiled at us, waved at us.

There was jazz in the bar. Real jazz. The unplanned kind that came from the soul and swept out the darkest corners of the mind of the person that invited it in. The kind of jazz that showed you your mess and made you like it just a bit. Made you find the beauty and the blessing in it.

We sat at a high top. The table just big enough to hold two glasses and force our elbows to bump and dance and meet again and again, introductions be damned.

We talked. I couldn't tell you what we talked about. The strange life of Robert Johnson and what we would do if we met the devil at a crossroads. We talked about how no one believed in time travel even though they'd seen other worlds and met a galaxies worth of people thanks to simple little books.

We talked until the bartender said it was done, and then we talked an hour more because she became interested in our conversation despite herself and took us to the bar so she could listen, and laugh, and talk herself as she cleaned.

He mopped. He took the mop from the bartender's hands and mopped her floor. He took off my shoes when the floor was dry and dared me to run across it so he would know it was really clean. I did. He said I was all arms and legs. He said he should have known I would be fast. Then he took his own shoes off and we raced: me, him, the bartender. From the door of the bar to the street. To see if we could.

We laughed when we cleaned the dirt from our feet.

I looked at him and got thankful for the night. Thankful for the moment. He felt like my best friend, and it all felt like a gift I would never be grateful enough for.

I carried that night with me every second of every day for a week. A full week. And then I saw him again. In Zegna.

FOUR

Cassidy

OH, I liked a man in custom Italian. It was always a touch more decadent than the situation called for. And Cahir was tailored within an inch of his life.

He unbuttoned his jacket and then his arms were around me, lifted me. I was so high in the air that things smelled different. I squealed like a child with a present and was glad Delia was at lunch with Colton. Glad that Nadia and O'Shea loved minding their own business more than anything in the world.

"Hello." He smiled.

I knew that smile. I knew it like he knew mine. And since our smiles were friends I gave him mine and let them meet again. "Hello."

"You got things for me?" His hands were on my shoulders. Heavy. That was good. Reassuring.

"Yep." I broke away from him, but felt him follow, steps in sync with mine, to the rack I filled for him.

"This." We said it together. We pointed at the same suit. Oh, I liked him. I liked him very much.

"You'll make everyone look so-"

"Everyone but you," he said. "You're always color."

Someone else would have corrected him, would have told him he forgot a word or three. But I heard him. Agreed. And wished he would shut up.

"Come with me." He stepped closer. "Come with me, Cassidy. I need a date. I want you to be-I want to take you on a date."

I might have said yes. I might have held onto the smile that was his smile's friend if I hadn't heard his footsteps shuffle and falter when he came into the office. Because he was looking at the space that used to be Zion's. And he didn't sigh, but I saw it build in his chest. I saw him pull it apart.

"No." I gave him the suit. "Have fun though. You'll have fun."

∞

Cahir

THE FIRST TIME I saw Zion it was like lightning struck my body.

I read my mother's romance novels when I was younger. I thought they would tell me all the things I didn't understand about girls. And I remember I read something like that in one of her books. It stuck with me when everything else about those books faded away. I thought it sounded unpleasant. Who wanted to be struck by lightening? I prayed it never happened to me.

Then I saw Zion, and it did happen to me. I found that

it was right. It was unpleasant to be singed from the tallest hair on my head to the tips of my feet. Ha. Unpleasant. It hurt like a bitch. But she'd already captured me, compelled me. I went to the source of the pain and like a mother with a newborn baby forgot that I was hurt in the first place.

Cassidy wasn't like that. The sight of her didn't hit me like lightening, but I saw her, in one glance, and knew that she contained lightening and fire. The kind that we harnessed for electricity and used to warm us on cold nights. The good things.

That night at the charity party, I saw the way her lightening could hurt. I saw the man that she pushed away without raising her arms, and I liked it. I thought about standing there, just out of sight, body leaned against the wall. I could have watched the show all night. But the man didn't look like he deserved lightening and fire. Or maybe I was greedy and famished to feel those things again. So I got her.

Her hand in mine felt like finding some place new.

I never danced with Zion. She shook her head every time music came on. She tucked her chin and smiled. Except for the one time she took me home. She danced with her mother and her aunts. Even then she was contained.

Cassidy was the wind. I saw the evidence of her and felt her and didn't know what she would do next and knew better than to try and contain her.

I didn't remember or recognize my laughter when it burst out of me. But I knew hers. By the end of that night, I knew her. I felt like I knew her better than anyone, and I didn't know what to do with it. I didn't know what to do with a perfect night. I didn't know what to do with myself besides wish for another one of them.

I didn't know my voice when it came from my body and

went to her ears. Didn't know what possessed me to ask her on a date. Then I found the yearning to connect with her again. To feel that kind of magic again. She had magic. Maybe a witch was safer than a siren.

She said no.

No.

When was the last time a woman said no to me?

Was what Zion did its own kind of no?

No usually made me mad. But Cassidy's no made me heavy. Made my face a different kind of sad. Lugubrious, even. Because I felt the sad on her. I almost saw it drape over her shoulders.

Of course. She would feel the absence inside me. She would do the right thing.

I left with a garment bag draped over my arm. I gave Junie the smile and wink I always had for her.

"She's off at four," Junie said. "Come back and get it right."

I didn't bother to ask how Junie heard. I didn't know how any of the women in that building did the things they did. I just respected their gifts.

I took Junie's words and held them close. I turned them over and over in my head until I found the place they were supposed to fit.

Okay, I said. I grabbed my car keys.

Cassidy had the last of her things stacked together. The music was quieter, different. The corner where she did her photography was clean of footprints and empty wine glasses.

"Hello," she said. She didn't turn around.

"Hello." I smiled. "I'm going to ask again."

"Why?"

"Because the question has changed a bit."

"Then you aren't really asking again, are you?" She faced me.

I sent a smile to meet hers because it was what I wanted most. "Will you come out with me? To the event? I could use a friend and another perfect night."

"A friend?"

"Yeah. Sorry I put the other stuff on you. It was-"

"I didn't ask for an apology. I don't think you should have given it. At least the other stuff wasn't sloppy or heavy."

I laughed. "Okay." I laughed again. "So. Will you?"

"As friends?"

"Or strangers if it makes you more comfortable."

She laughed. "Are we friends, Cahir?"

"There were a few times that night that I thought we were best friends."

"Yes." She nodded and all that hair bounced. "I thought so too."

I wanted to press another "So?" I wanted to push more insistence her way. But I knew it wouldn't do me any good, and I didn't know how I knew what I knew. I put my hands in my pockets. And waited.

"Okay. I have a dress. I'll go."

"Thanks, friend."

We laughed together.

She hefted a heavy bag onto her shoulder. "Come have a drink with Junie and I."

"Oh, I don't want to-"

"You might as well. Since you're letting her send you back here to pressure me."

If I were sorry, I wouldn't have grinned. "Okay."

∞

Cahir

IT WAS the opening of an art exhibition. I didn't care much about it. Didn't care much about art at all. Not that I could tell Zion that. She would have dragged me all over O'Shea's gallery space. I would have enjoyed it. I found myself wandering it sometimes. I even bought one of her pieces. A small thing, just a hand. Zion didn't have to tell me the hand was hers. No one did. I would always recognize her, see her.

I didn't know where I put the painting after-After. But it was gone. And I was at the opening with Cassidy. She wore black and slashed with red. Slashed it across her eyes, cheeks, and lips. Slid it onto her feet and the soles of her shoes. She should have looked like a bruise, a pimple that wanted to be popped, a clown. Instead she looked like a volcano when the first of the lava reached for the sky. She looked like forest fires. She looked like suffocation.

It caught me. For a few milliseconds, it froze me. Then she smiled. We looked at the art. She whispered her thoughts. Some nice. Some naughty. Some made me bend at the waist and laugh so hard I thought after the ground, the floor, swallowed it that it would vibrate and send the energy back to me.

Irreverent. I didn't know how she could take herself so seriously and not at all. I wished she would teach me.

She knew everyone I knew. And when she told them that we were friends, not "just friends," but friends, they all accepted it. We drank cheap red wine and competed to see who could make the most ridiculous face. We ate hors d'oeuvres and then gave up and hoarded a tray between us.

I was light again.

I missed drowning.

When it was time to leave, she pulled out a wad of cash and handed it to the curator, pointed.

"Wow, cash money." I rolled the words around in my mouth while she laughed. "Cash. Cash?"

She nodded. "I like it."

"Me too. Come on, Cash. Let's go."

"I'm driving."

Idiot that I was, I gave her the keys. She pushed my Range Rover through the streets like it was a Lamborghini.

"That was fun." She gave the keys and a smile to valet.

"Was it?" My ankle buzzed when I put my weight on it. My whole body buzzed.

"Come on. You'll feel human when I put some alcohol in you."

"Maybe."

She laughed.

We walked two flights of stairs to get to the bar that despised children and families but stocked all the board games from my youth on the community tables. As if anyone could see the Monopoly board in the dark.

There was always a fire in one of the two fireplaces. A small, dancing fire from the gas fireplace on one side of the bar in the summer. A roaring wood fire on the other side in the winter.

We sat at another of those tables too small for strangers and too big for us. Gin for me. Vodka for her. A basket of fries and a small plate of meatballs between us that she cut into an even number of pieces.

"You don't want to argue with me, Cahir," she said in the middle of her task.

And then I did, just a little bit, to see what it would be like to be struck by her brand of lightening and eaten by her fire.

"What kind of name is Cahir anyways?" She licked ketchup off her finger.

The fries did look good. "Irish. My dad's Irish."

"Is he?" She raised an eyebrow.

"He and my mom."

"I'm not going to drag it out of you."

"Good. I like this suit."

"You'd better."

We laughed.

"I'm adopted," I said.

"How does that feel?"

"It's-" I put my elbows on the table and shook my head. "Fuck me. No one's ever asked me that. It doesn't feel like anything most days. Some days it's odd. If I'm in a room with other Chinese people. They'll speak to me, and I won't be able to answer. They shake their heads, and Cash, it feels like I've betrayed parents I've never had and a culture I've never known."

"Do you want it?"

"The parents or the culture?"

"You have parents."

"Yeah." I laughed. "Shit, Cash. Okay. I can do this. Okay."

"Wanna stretch or something?"

"I don't miss the culture. I was never interested in how to be the right kind of Chinese. It was never a thing. I spent my life surrounded by white people unless I sought out something else. Culture didn't matter. Money did."

"Mmm."

I didn't know if it was my words that made her hum or the food in her mouth. "Everyone that looked at me already assumed I was smarter, better, richer, more educated, more cultured, just because of what I looked like. Why put more work into it?"

"Huh."

"Could you live without yours?"

"My culture? God, no. If I lost being a Black woman, the community that comes with it, I would cut off my arms. It would mean the same thing."

"Yeah?"

"So many things I don't have to say and so many ways I'm understood. Just because I walked in the room. I see Black women and I see family. I'm family as soon as they see me. And we speak the same language. Whether we grew up in the whitest neighborhood or the blackest. A few sentences and then it clicks and we're all speaking the same language and moving our bodies the same way."

"Just Black women? Not men?"

She shook her head, and I knew I was an outsider. I knew to back away.

We ate fries. I ordered us more. Another round of drinks. The silence was full. It didn't need my help. It didn't need my contributions. I let it rest until the words had to spill out of me.

"Can I tell you about Zion?"

FIVE

Cahir

SHE LOOKED up from her drink. The little candle on our table made all of the red on her face and the brown of her eyes...I wished I had the words. I cursed myself for lacking the words.

"I wish someone would," she said.

I laughed. And I told her. About the bookstore where we had our first date and the cookbooks and the abortion that she had without me, that made her leave me. About the split and the reconciliation that wasn't a reconciliation to Zion because there was no baby and then how we split again. I told her about graceful hands and a soft voice and eyes darker than midnight and as bottomless as hell. I told her what it was like to lay next to Zion at night and what it was like to lay alone. I told her about the secret place that I thought I wouldn't tell anyone else about.

"My therapist says it wasn't rape. Technically. Legally. It was sexual assault." It was easier to watch the flame of the candle flicker and twist than to watch Cash's eyes. "I say I showered fifteen times in three days and didn't know what I was trying to wash off."

"Cahir." Her voice was warm and soft.

I didn't know how to tell her that was worse. Compassion and understanding were worse.

"I have a lot of good friends. I collect them in my business. Mainly by accident. And when I told them why Zion was gone. The men-" I shook my head. "They jumped back like I had a contagious disease. Every single one of them was horrified. Every single woman told me to get over it, to forgive her. Maybe go to counseling with her. It was just holes in a condom. I could get over it. Zion was amazing, and we were in love."

"Hmm."

I looked up because I had to know. Her lips were pursed and her eyes were slits.

"I found the words eventually to explain to them that it felt like my body didn't belong to me. She made me feel like my body was just there to...do what she wanted. I didn't get to say yes or no. I didn't get a say in my own life or what I did. I didn't matter enough to get a say. She would do what she wanted, and I would fall in line." I rolled a cold French fry between my fingers. "I got the words to tell them how it felt to love someone and know that no matter what they said or the pain they were going through, they didn't give a shit about you. If they did, they wouldn't have betrayed you in the first place."

"I'm sorry."

I put the fry down. Wiped my hands. "I am too."

∞

Cahir

CASH NEVER GAVE me her cell phone number. Maybe it was because I didn't ask. But I didn't want to. Every time I spent more than five minutes with her, there was magic. Perfection. The comfortable kind I could sit in for a while. For a while, I wasn't drowning. I missed drowning, missed being in the ocean, fighting, arms and legs heavy, to get closer to the siren that sang for me.

My assistant got Cash's number for me. I held the piece of paper she wrote it on in my hands and felt the sweat break out under my arms. I laughed at myself. It was just Cash. It was just a phone call.

The phone barely rang.

"It's not that weird that you found my number."

I leaned back in my chair, smile already too wide on my face. But I couldn't help it or stop it. I could hear her smile. "Oh, yeah?"

"You do all that weird tech stuff. Your office is probably full of weird gadgets and stuff. Like in cartoons."

I laughed and looked around at my office. Minimal like everything else in my life. I hated clutter. I hated other people's ideas pressing in on me.

"Shit." She sighed. "I hate being wrong."

I laughed again. "Be my friend."

"I already am. Your best one."

The smile was going to break my face. "Prove it. Have lunch with me."

I didn't have to see her to know she rolled her eyes, to know the smile was still there. "Send me an address."

So I did. I went to the food hall when I wasn't sure what I wanted to eat but knew I wanted sunshine, old school rap, hipster kids, and business people that wanted beers while they had their meetings. And I thought Cash would like it.

She was covered in flowers. They were on her dress. On

her rings and her earrings. There was one braided in her hair. Combat boots on her feet. I shook my head.

"Yes," she said. "I do look wonderful. Thank you."

"You're welcome." I hugged her and realized. She never smelled the same. It was like her scent changed to match her outfits. She smelled like honey suckle and lilies that day.

We got food. Found a booth to squeeze into. She raised an eyebrow. I rolled my eyes and got us drinks.

"I talked to my mom today," she said.

"Oh, yeah?"

"Yeah. She's-" Cash shrugged. "I'm a disappointment to her."

"Shut the fuck up." I didn't mean for my mouth to hang open. No one wanted to see a half chewed piece of salmon. But I couldn't help it.

And I guess it helped. She laughed.

"My grandmother has always owned her own business, made her own money. My parents did the same. Real estate development in Baltimore. They like that I do something 'artsy and free'. They don't get why I've got to work for someone else."

"Ah. The shitty thing about entrepreneurs."

"Yeah." She tilted her head.

"Okay." My chopsticks picked through my poke bowl until I found a scallop. "Entrepreneurship is weird. Everyone thinks it's owning your own business, right?"

"Right."

"I've always disagreed with that. Owning a business isn't enough. Entrepreneurship it's-it's a spirit, right? It's this desire to take ownership of a thing and make it grow." I found another scallop and put it on her plate. "I can't run companies with people that want to be cogs in a machine or just want to clock in and clock out, collect a paycheck. They have to be people that look at my companies and see them as their own, they have to buy into them as if they've got everything on the line too. They do have everything on the line. They've staked their reputation and skills on the fact that they can make this work. Cause if it doesn't work, they're screwed. I can find someone else to give me money. Shit, I've made enough. I can fund my own ventures. They'll have to throw their resumé with all their failed projects around and hope that someone takes mercy on them."

"Oh my God."

"Look at your resumé. You worked for the Agency from the first day they opened their doors. You left when you saw they were stagnating and decided to work for an ex-escort in a building owned by a former sugar baby. You decided to gamble. Maybe you don't want to own a business. But you sure like building them."

I bent my head over my food. I loved seaweed. I was ashamed of that as a kid: how much I liked Asian food even though I didn't give a shit about being Asian. It was a friend that told me to get my head out of my ass. Good food was good food.

"Oh my God."

Cash hadn't touched her food. Thai. I liked Thai.

"I have to call my mom." She ran out of the food hall.

Her lunch was delicious. The joy on her face, the kind that only shows up when you're understood, was even better.

∞

Cassidy

IT WASN'T FUNNY. It wasn't funny. It wasn't funny. I
threw my head back and laughed like a hyena anyways. I
knew horror movies weren't supposed to be funny. Slasher
films weren't supposed to be funny. There was music and
lighting and back story set up to surprise and shock and stun
viewers into silence. But so much of it was wrong. They
didn't research the spirits or the magic they used. Millions
of dollars to spend and they couldn't hire someone to teach
them about the other worlds. They just made things up.

And how many deaths could be avoided if there was
just a little common sense? How many of those films
weren't even about a real plot? How many of them just
wanted to see how many gruesome ways there were to die
in ninety-four minutes?

I watched "scary" movies when my brain needed a
break, when I'd watched the same fashion show for the
fifteenth time, when I'd called the same designer for the
twentieth time, when a shipment was delayed. Again. They
reminded me that the world was ridiculous, that I was
ridiculous, and I could laugh loud if I wanted to.

I couldn't think of a better way to spend a Saturday
evening. Company would have been nice. Not that my
plants didn't count as company. They were some of the best
friends I had. But they couldn't laugh with me.

I turned my phone over in my hands and crossed my
legs on my couch. Junie wouldn't come. She said scary
movies were actually scary and there was something wrong
with me that medication wouldn't fix. My grandmother was
busy. She was always busy. It didn't seem fair to call her
away from her store and all the prep work she had. I should
have gone to help her.

There was Cahir. I knew if I called he would answer. I
knew if I asked he would come. Our days fell into a pattern.

We had lunch together three or four times a week. Once or twice a week he would have drinks with Junie and I. We went to all of the interesting events together. I even dragged him to New York Fashion Week with me. Delia went to all of the higher end designer's shows. I trawled for the lesser knowns. The ones with talent and no budget. He took me to tech conferences and told me when it was okay to lean my head on his shoulder and fall asleep. I told myself it was best to not enjoy how he looked onstage in the clothes I picked for him too much.

We were friends.

We were friends! I rolled my eyes at myself, at the way I overthought the simplest of things and called him.

"I'll be there in twenty minutes," he said. "Pick something good. I want to see a lot of people die."

I laughed. And changed into something a bit more appropriate.

SIX

Cassidy

"WOW." His eyes were slow. Slow and heavy as they dragged over my baggy sweats and faded, shapeless t-shirt, my bonnet. "You really just wanted to watch a movie."

"Did you wear sweatpants to my house, you whore?"

He held up a plastic bag. "There's jeans and popcorn in here."

I laughed and let him in.

"Holy shit." He froze a few feet from the door.

I forgot, I always forgot, what my apartment looked like to newcomers. I forgot how the fiddle leaf fig and the cactus, a few feet away from touching the nine foot ceilings, the jade plant, the bamboo between the windows, the two lemon trees that flanked the television, the young oak tree in its large glass pot full of water, the succulents on the coffee table, the rosemary, mint, basil, and lavender that crowded the windowsill all caught people by surprise. But wasn't it natural to want to be natural? To have only a few pieces of furniture in pale colors or just white, to bring in natural woods, and thick rugs so that the plants could shine?

"This makes perfect sense." He tossed a smile over his shoulder at me.

Where his smiles were usually light, that one fell heavy and made something inside me thud just once.

"I'm going to change." He tossed a box of popcorn and a large bag of peanut M&M's at me. "Get the provisions ready."

I laughed.

That laughter died when he sprawled on the couch beside me and dumped the peanut M&M's into the popcorn.

"What is wrong with you?"

"Sweet, salty, and savory all at once." He shoved a handful into his mouth and smiled. Chocolate stained his teeth.

I rolled my eyes and started the movie. He jumped while I laughed. He closed his eyes while I scoffed at the absurdity. He screamed once and didn't look offended when I laughed so hard I cried.

Shadows fell long across the floor until only the television provided light and washed the color from his face.

"Thanks for coming over." Every moment we spent together felt like another perfect moment, like something snatched out of a movie. There was no reason for me to feel awkward. "I used to do this with Kevin a lot."

He handed me the bowl of popcorn and chocolate. I took a handful. I didn't know how to tell him it was a good idea, a good movie snack.

"You never talk about him."

I crossed my legs and pushed my hair back. "I met Kevin on a Thursday. Thursdays were our days. Always.

We always did something together. We always ended up in bed. Or doing the things adults do in bed."

I liked the way Cahir grinned. Like he got it because he'd done it. "Where'd you meet?"

"He owns nightclubs. I went to one. No. I snuck into one. They were already at capacity, but I knew I was supposed to be there. I was supposed to dance there that night. I decided the best place for me to go after I made it into the club was the DJ booth."

Cahir laughed.

"He was there. He saw me dancing. He said that was what made him stop. Not that I was beautiful. The way I danced."

"Yeah. I get that."

"He stood to the side of the booth and just watched me dance. Then I went to him. And from then on it felt like I never left him." I shrugged. "It was one of those-Like a hurricane. There would be a little calm and then we would go out and rage. Wreak destruction on whatever we could find. We wanted the whole world. To see it all. Mark it all. Do something vulgar to it."

"Sounds exhausting."

I tilted my head. "Yeah. It was. In a way. But he made tired feel good, natural. I didn't need to keep my eyes open when I wasn't with him anyways."

"Shit."

"Shit," I said."

"So how'd you find out?"

"It was a Thursday." I laughed at the irony of it. "He came to me and when he put his arms around me there was something else there. I sniffed and sniffed and sniffed, and the more I did the more the dread grew in my chest. A knot of it. It didn't matter what incense or herbs I lit. It didn't matter how much I danced or fucked. It was there. Right there."

"Damn, Cash."

"I followed him and wondered how I could get so deep with a man that I knew when his smell changed. He went only two blocks from here. He met his wife for coffee only two blocks from the bed he left me in. My bed." I shook my head. There were tears the day I discovered his other life, that I was the other life. I let them come until there were none left, until I was sure I would never cry again. "It was worse because I could see that he loved her, worshipped her. Worse because I could see she loved him, but she was like me. She could smell that something was different. But she wouldn't follow. It would drive her insane."

He wrapped his hand around mine. "Fuck 'em. Fuck both of them."

I looked down at the scars on his hand. Half a smile. The sad smile. "Yeah. Fuck 'em."

∞

Cahir

WHEN I TOLD Cash about Zion, I felt like origami. A whole thing that folded in on itself over and over and over again until something small and visually pleasing and less than was left. When she told me about Kevin, she expanded until I wondered if I would choke. Everything was pushed out. Everything but her.

There was no sorrow. No anger. No shame. Just a fullness that said she was whole and right. Someone to be feared. I was grateful all over again that she was my friend. I was reminded all over again that nothing was stronger than a woman who decided survival was beneath her-she would thrive.

I knew what happened to her and what happened to me were different. She was lied to. She was spun into a world that didn't exist where others could see. I was...violated. And that still made my stomach turn. I still shook my head and tried to point to all the ways Zion was broken and not really to blame. But when I pointed it was with less conviction.

I didn't know what that meant.

I thought about it in the car when I drove home. I thought about it in the elevator and when I walked down the hall to my apartment. I thought so hard I didn't see. I almost tripped over them: a book and Tupperware. Still warm. I opened it. Pasta. Hand cut. Uneven. Fatter in some places than others. It smelled good. And wasn't that a bitch?

There was a book. A biography. Those were the books I picked out for her when she took me back to her book store, the one she took me to on that first date. Stories of people as powerful as she was. She would give them back to me and ask me to read them as well, to read the parts that interested her. I flipped open the book and tried to keep the popcorn and M&M's down. Yes. There was her handwriting, small and fine, in the margins.

I went into my apartment and dumped it all on the kitchen counter. I fished my phone out of my pocket. Cash. Cash would understand.

"I don't miss you, Cahir. Jesus."

It would have made me laugh any other time. I knew it was supposed to make me laugh. "She was here. She left pasta. And a book."

The silence dragged, and I was drowning again. It was familiar. Welcome.

"Are you hungry?"

I laughed. Because I was surprised. Because I wasn't drowning for just a second.

"If you aren't hungry, throw it away. Throw away the book too."

I looked at the bowl. "I am a little hungry."

She sighed. "Then eat, Cahir. I hope it makes you feel better."

"It won't."

She hung up.

I was a coward. The worst kind.

SEVEN

Cahir

"YOU'VE GOT thirty minutes to get dressed." Cash hung up the phone.

I stared at it. She woke me out of the Zion dream. At the wrong place-the happy place. When all I could feel was the squeeze of her body as she pulled me deeper into her, eyes open to stare into mine and banish me from my own reality. I didn't need that. I needed to wake with the anger and the shock. It was the only way I could lay still and feel justified about being in my bed alone. It was the only way I stopped myself from reaching for her.

My phone pinged with an address and a message: *twenty-seven minutes*.

I laughed. It took me twenty minutes to get dressed and fifteen to drive to the address she gave me.

I parked under the bridge and stepped out of my car. I looked around until I saw her reddish-brown halo of hair.

"Farmer's market?"

She peeked at me over her sunglasses. "We should do something about how hungry you are."

I almost cried. I threw an arm around her shoulders. "You're a good friend, Cash."

"Your best one." She bumped me with her hip. "Let's go."

The market sprawled out under the heavy overpass. Box trucks ringed the outside with the names of farms blazoned on their sides. Oil popped and sizzled. There was the scrape of metal spatulas on griddles. Long plastic and wooden tables and large colorful signs.There was laughter and children and their tired but happy parents. There were couples and groups of friends. There was Cash and I.

We didn't start with food. I bought her a purse and didn't know when I took my wallet out. I had a lemonade with something that made me widen my eyes. She laughed at me.

"Elderflower, mint, a little lemon. Auntie Beulah does it right," she said.

"Auntie?"

"A friend of my grandmother's."

"What's your grandmother like? You talk about her a lot."

"I should. She's my favorite. I barely had to ask her to let me have the apartment over her shop."

I blinked. I knew she lived over a store. I never asked whose store it was. Never cared. There was parking and a set of steps that led up to Cash's apartment. The store didn't matter. Dumb of me. "What kind of shop?"

Cash wagged her finger. "Uh-uh. We're not here to talk about me."

"But it's fun." I put a little petulance and whine into my voice and hoped she would-

Yeah. She laughed. That was good. Real good.

"I want to know-"

"I'll tell you," I said.

"I know you will." She led me over to a table full of flowers. I didn't think she realized she wandered to it. She ran her hands over the flowers, buried her face in them, smiled at them.

I slipped the florist cash and pointed at two of the bigger buckets. She beamed at me. I put a finger to my lips and mouthed that I would come back to get them. Like I had to go back and get a pallet of little succulents and tomato vines that Cash cooed over the way most women cooed over babies.

I didn't recognize myself.

I didn't know if I was grateful for that or miserable.

"What do you want to know?"

She looked up from the flowers. There was pollen on her nose. I brushed it away. And I brushed away the urge that came to me.

"I want to play pretend." She looped an arm around my waist and picked up the basket we hadn't put a single bit of food in.

"What are we pretending?"

"That tomorrow we're letting Zion and Kevin back into our lives."

Two things burst in my chest- the hope I kept buried because it was foolish, dumb, would probably get me killed and the wrongness of Cash going back to that man.

"Tell me what it's like to have Zion back."

We went to a table heavy with root vegetables. We didn't talk. Just picked up sweet, red, and purple potatoes. Golden beets. She pulled out her money. I put it in my pocket and paid.

"Zion's back." I took the basket out of Cash's hands. She put tomatoes in it. "Okay. Um. Zion's back."

"You can do it."

Could I? I closed my eyes and stood still. Blocked out the scent of Cash's perfume. Vanilla and caramel and maybe apples.

"It's quieter. Muted. Tight like violin strings." I shake my head. "I feel like my head's under water, and I'm probably going to drown in all the shit I'm feeling. Part of me is relieved that she's back. Part of me is angry with myself for being so weak. I took her back. She broke me and didn't try to fix me, fix us, fix herself. But I took her back. I told her it was all okay. Again. How will she break me this time?"

Cash's fingers were slim and long. Cool when they slipped between mine. I put apples and pears in the basket. Blackberries. Odd. Blackberry season should have been over.

"That's what I think when I wake up in the morning." I smiled when Cash pulled my wallet out of my pocket for me. I pointed to the card I wanted to use. She put my wallet back in my pocket and after she signed the receipt she kept the card and put her hand back in mine.

"What do you think?"

I liked the color of her eyes. We walked through patches of sun that lit them up. Cinnamon brown. As spicy as her personality and as warm as her laugh. The perfect match to the freckles over her cheeks and nose.

I shook my head. "How will she break me this time? She's contained. I've always known it, but now I always see it. Every time she touches her stomach I want to force a pregnancy test in her hands. But I don't want to know. If she's pregnant, she'll keep it, and I'll really drown. I can't be a father."

"Why not?"

I pushed her hair out of her face when she wouldn't look up at me.

She laughed and pushed my hand away. "What? I think you'd be a dope father."

"Maybe." I shrugged. "Probably."

She laughed again.

"Before, it was that I was busy. When I have a family, I want to be able to come home at the same time every day. I want to be there on weekends. I want to be there for games and practices. For nights when they're still a baby and won't sleep. Chicken pox."

"Do kids still get that?"

"Fuck. I don't know. But I want to be there. I don't want to be the one that shows up with just money. I want to be a parent. I want to actually raise my child."

"And you can't right now?"

"No. I'm stretched in too many directions, too many places. Too many people depending on me. And I love it. I don't want to stop yet. A couple years?" I shrugged.

"I'd have to leave her. I'd have to leave a kid." I shook my head. "Or there's no baby and I watch it pull her apart from the inside out. Now we're drowning together and there's shit I can do to stop it. She won't help herself. Not in a way that fixes it. She just decides and does. Fuck me and if it hurts me or kills my happiness."

Cash rubbed the hand that held hers. Rubbed the fingers I turned mottled pink and white.

I loosened my grip a little. There was shame in that, shame that I couldn't let go. But when I tried her fingers tightened over mine. I looked into her eyes. She was my friend. My best one.

"I um-" I sighed. "There would be some magic

moments. Maybe the sex would be what it used to be."

"Men." Cash rolled her eyes.

I laughed. I never laughed when I talked about Zion. "But I'd spend almost the entire time angry and disgusted with myself for letting her back in my life after what she did."

"What would you be doing the rest of the time?"

"Worrying if she were pregnant and terrified that she was going to poke more holes in condoms or do something else to make me feel like I wasn't even important enough to have a say."

She stopped me. In between the donut cart and the gyro stall. She hugged me. Arms tight around my neck and her whole body flush to mine. Hair in my nose. I put the basket at my feet and wrapped my arms around her waist, waist so small I thought I could probably encircle it with my hands. Everything about her was so small. And yet she took up every available space in my mind in that moment. She took up all the air and replaced it with something I liked better and couldn't name. I closed my eyes and prayed that we could stay like that forever or at least a lifetime or two.

She loosened her arms when someone bumped into us. They muttered a hurried apology when they saw her face.

Her hand came to my cheek. I leaned into it and kept my eyes on hers. I hoped and waited for her to just tip her head back and-

Because I couldn't do it. And I didn't know why.

Instead her hand slid back into mine. I picked up the basket and stepped out of the sun with her.

"What would it be like if Kevin came back?"

She shook her head. "Kevin isn't coming back, Cahir."

It was a long while before I remembered to breathe again.

EIGHT

Cahir

"HOW CAN you live in a place that doesn't have a single plant?" Cash slid mushrooms into the pan.

Things changed after the farmer's market. Not in any kind of dramatic way. Our routine just tilted, slipped, a little bit. We cooked after the farmer's market in her kitchen. She turned on some producer from Brazil and bopped around her kitchen. Loose hips and long arms that called then screamed at me until I was there with her. We ate. The next day when I called her about lunch she sent me a recipe. I grabbed the ingredients and was at her apartment, grateful that we could have so much control over our schedules.

It was easy to be in the kitchen with her. Our knives never clashed and our hands never reached for the same things. I learned her music and sang along with her. We danced while fish and seafood simmered. While chicken thighs were weighed down and made the oil pop in protest.

We never made pasta.

I shrugged and stirred the mushrooms until they were all coated in butter. "I never thought about it. I've killed so many plants."

"Murderer." She bumped my hip with hers so I would know she was joking.

"My problem is I want to give them too much love. I water and water and water them even though I don't have to, even though they didn't ask for it."

"Hmm. How interesting."

I shook my head. "Shut up."

"Shutting."

I laughed and took over stirring the rice.

She sprinkled salt and cracked pepper over the mushrooms and grated more parmesan into the rice. "I can't remember the last time I had risotto. I'm excited."

"I'll be excited if we don't fuck it up."

She grinned. "We don't fuck things up."

And we didn't. I sat across from her at the dining table that I never used in the studio apartment that was all concrete and way too much space and poured us wine. I watched her eyes slide shut when she took the first bite. I grinned when she danced in her chair and thought of all the other kinds of risotto we could make, the other things I could cook without her help that would make her dance like that.

I wanted to move. I wanted to sit beside her and have the most awkward meal of my life because I kept her left hand in my right. We didn't even need to talk. I just wanted her skin against mine. I wanted to press my ear to her chest to hear her heart beat and her voice before it was released from her body.

I really didn't recognize myself.

"Come to a thing with me this weekend," I said.

"Okay. What's the thing?" Her eyes didn't leave the risotto.

"Casual. Just some food. Friends."

"Here?"

"No." I cleared my throat. "My parent's house."

There were her eyes. Wide with alarm. "You want me to meet your parents?"

"I want you to hang out with me and my friends on my parent's back deck while I take over my father's grill and smoker."

"Ugh. A smoker."

"I'm thinking about smoking some fish."

"A snapper. We could stuff it with something."

"Grill some crabs?"

Her eyes were wide with amazement, curiosity. "I've never had grilled crabs before."

"I baste them in a butter Old Bay sauce."

"I love Old Bay."

"Of course you do, Baltimore."

She laughed. "Fine. You've bribed me well. I'll meet your parents."

∞

Cassidy

HE PICKED me up and smiled at my outfit. "You look like O'Shea."

"Do I?" I looked down at my mom jeans, crop top, and favorite Doc Martens. "Crabs come with their own dress code. I don't make the rules."

He laughed and pulled away from my apartment. We went to the supermarket. Then the farmer's market.

Then the wharf. My hand rested in his almost the entire time.

I liked it. Liked that that was where our friendship was. I slipped a hand into Junie's once. I looped my arm through hers. She shook me loose and said she needed both hands free in case "someone ran up on us."

Cahir reached for my hand sometimes, and I didn't realize it. It was that natural to me. Or he threw an arm around my shoulders and I only wondered why it took him so long to do it. Sometimes he smiled down at me. Just smiled. Sometimes he looked at me, and I didn't want to ask what the looks meant.

Whenever I gathered the courage to ask, he was Cahir again and there was laughter between us, sunshine between us, something precious.

He drove us to the home he grew up in. A sprawling, graceful brick Tudor with ivy and a garden that made my grin break into a smile.

"I thought you'd like that," he said.

I was out of the car, my head bent to smell the eucalyptus that must have been a labor of love to grow. "I can't believe you kill plants."

"It was my one great failing as a mother," a soft, lilting voice said.

I knew Cahir was adopted. We talked about it more than once. And still the strawberry-blond woman with her open smile was a surprise to me.

"I'm Maeve." She came to me with her arms open.

I stepped into them. "I'm Cassidy."

"Oh, sweet darling, I know. He told me he was bringing a friend I hadn't met before, and I pumped him for information. Cahir's had the same friends since high school."

"I made a few in college." He walked around his Range

Rover with the styrofoam cooler full of crabs.

"Exactly that." Maeve laughed. "A few. And they're both inside waiting for you."

Cahir rolled his eyes and kissed Maeve's cheek. "They're here to stare at you. And drink Dad's beer."

"Sure and it's only high quality beer I bring into the house, isn't it?"

I blinked. The booming voice belonged to a black haired man that could have told me he was an Irish god. I wouldn't have questioned him.

"Jack." He folded me into his arms. "There can never be too many beautiful women in this house. I'm glad my son brought another."

I grinned. "Flattery will you get you everywhere, Jack."

He threw back his head and laughed then tossed an arm over me and Maeve's shoulders. "But I'm already where I want to be."

"Snake charmer." Maeve rolled her eyes.

"Cahir, how come you aren't as smooth as your father?" I was only a few steps behind him.

Not that it mattered. I would have felt the dirty look he threw over his shoulder from a mile away.

Inside the house was cool and bright and open. Cut flowers were everywhere. Art too. The furniture was large and comfortable. Each room moved smoothly from one to the other. It was a family home. The kind that embraced you and whispered in your ear how happy it was that you were there.

His friends were in the kitchen. A mix of men and women whose names I forgot as soon as Cahir introduced them to me. Not that I had a chance to talk to them. As soon as the food was brought in from the car, I was beside him at the counter.

We fell into the pattern, the dance, of creating a meal together. It was soothing, natural, fun. He put on my favorite playlist and sang with me, danced around and past his friends with me in an impromptu meringue. We laughed at jokes that had grown so many layers we couldn't explain them if we wanted to.

And his friends watched. First with their faces open and welcoming. Then with surprise and incredulity. The surprise and incredulity were focused on me.

Zion, I thought. I'm not her. They want to know why I'm here.

But no. I scented and touched the vibes that were thrown at me. I teased and tasted them and thought they were familiar but could not figure out why.

I helped Cahir at the grill. I helped Maeve set the table and didn't understand her smiles. I carried food to the table or tried to and didn't understand why Jack was so gentle when he took the bowls and platters I carried from me. I didn't understand where his winks and smiles that made me giggle went.

I chewed on it until I had to put it aside for the food. I moaned into the crabs. I danced over the fish.

And then I understood. When my plate was never empty, I never ran out of napkins, my glass was always full. When Cahir picked another crab for me and beat one of his friends back from the last piece of fish and gave it to me. When his hand rested on the back of my chair and then my back. When he played in my hair or with my earrings. When I realized that he didn't notice any of what he did. He just...moved. He just adjusted his body so it was always in contact with mine.

Shit.

Fucking hell.

NINE

Cassidy

"SO WHAT THE fuck is going on with you?" Junie's gum smelled like strawberries.

I was on the third floor. We called it the "Lonely Third." All of that wide open space and there was nothing in the space but a few couches that O'Shea and Nadia threw up there for "interesting activities." I always sprayed the couches with sanitizer before I sat on them.

"What?"

"Don't play dumb, Cassidy." Junie sat down next to me and pulled her neon pink braids over her shoulder. "Cahir's been here twice today. Why you being a pussy?"

"I'm not being a pussy," I said.

Junie raised an eyebrow and popped her gum.

"Okay. Maybe I am. But you don't understand."

"No shit. Why do you think I'm up here?"

"Junie." I rolled my eyes.

"Cassidy." She rolled hers back and did a much better job.

"You have to teach me how to do that."

Junie turned to face me on the couch. "Nadia taught me. The secret is to move real slow. Like this."

I watched her iris move. "Okay. I can do that."

Twenty minutes later I thought my eyes were about to fall out of my head. And I remembered what it felt like to laugh.

"Great. You're all happy and bubbly again." Junie smiled. "Why you playing hide and seek with Cahir?"

"I went home with him over the weekend."

"Bout time you started fucking again. How'd you do?"

My mouth fell open. "How'd I do?"

"Oh, bitch, I can look at him and tell what that's going to be like. So yeah, how'd you do?"

"I went home with him like to where his parent's live."

"Oh. Boring. Should've fucked him instead."

I slapped her shoulder. "Will you focus?"

"I'm laser sharp, baby. And I said what I said. The dick would've been more fun."

"I don't know. We grilled crabs."

"Oh, shit. That sounds delightful."

I didn't mean to laugh as loud as I did. "It was. So was the way he made sure I always had food on my plate or a napkin or a drink. So was the way he played in my hair and rubbed my back and shoulders. So was the way he cracked my crabs for me."

"Oh, shit. He's in love."

"He is!" I jumped up and almost dropped my laptop on the ground. I swung it over my head before I remembered it was my work laptop and tossed it onto the couch. "Right? I didn't pick up on it at first."

"Because there was food."

"Yes. So much good food to make and then eat." God,

those crabs were magnificent. Basting them in a beer and butter sauce while they cooked was pure genius. "But I noticed them all looking at me crazy. And his mom smiling and his father stopped flirting with me."

"His dad was flirting with you? Ew. Unless he was fine. Then it gets a little more interesting."

I choked a bit. "Not like that, June. Like the way fathers do. You know? When it doesn't mean anything?"

"And he just stopped?"

"Yeah."

"That's a shame. I love threesomes with relatives."

"I don't even know you."

"You don't need to," Junie said. "So he's in love. What's up? Why you hiding?"

"I-" I stood in front of her with both hands in the air and my mouth open. "In love."

"Right."

"I don't understand why you don't understand."

Junie gave me another perfect eye roll. "He's your friend, right?"

"Yeah." I drew out the word.

"Your best one."

I shrugged.

Junie popped her gum.

"Fine. Yes, he is."

"I only find it mildly offensive that he's usurped me."

I grinned.

"If he's your best friend, and y'all cool like you say you are, why can't you just talk to him about it? At least get him to confirm it either way. Sitting up here with the dust and God knows what else is on this couch ain't going to help you either way."

"It's nice up here. Lots of light."

"Girl, shut up." Junie tossed her hair over her shoulder. "You being pussy, and I'm not going to tell you the shit's okay. And not that it matters, but if you're in the mood you could consider how it feels for him to have you one day and lose you the next and have no idea why it's happening."

Shame was a close and tight thing. Like Saran Wrap, it clung to me.

"You don't have to feel bad if you don't want to though." Junie blew a bubble. "Delia and O'Shea taught me there's power in not giving a shit what a man thinks or how he feels."

"No," I whispered. "He's my friend."

"You'll get better service if you call him downstairs," Junie said.

∞

Cassidy

I DIDN'T CALL HIM. I tossed my phone between my hands until I dropped it. My heart jumped into my throat until I was sure I hadn't cracked the screen.

I went home. I burned Palo Santo and rosemary. I sat on my couch with my rose quartz in my hands. I drank tea. I listened to Meshell Ndegeocello. I thought about watching a movie. I thought about how hungry I was and what I wanted for dinner. Cahir had leftovers. Cahir had crabs.

I got in my car and drove to his house.

He opened the door after the second knock. "I ate all of the crabs."

"Son of a bitch." I pushed past him and laid down on his couch. "I guess I deserved that."

"You did." He went into the kitchen. I heard the wine

glasses clink when he set them on the counter. The pull of the cork from the bottle.

He put a glass of wine on the coffee table in front of me then leaned against the back of the couch. "Gonna tell me what crawled up your ass and made you abandon me?"

"That's why I came over and now I don't want to do it."

"That bad?"

I threw an arm over my eyes and nodded. "Because I think I'm right. But what if I'm wrong? Then I'll look ridiculous and make our whole friendship weird. I don't want to make us weird."

"Me either. I like us the way we are. It's pretty fucking dope."

"It is!" I threw the arm over my eyes up in the air and let it fall over my eyes again.

"But-"

"I hate that there's a but," I said.

"Wouldn't it make us weird if you keep it to yourself and now we've got this big awkward thing between us that we can't talk about because you won't tell me what it is."

"Jesus fucking Christ." I took a deep breath. "I think you're falling in love with me."

The silence grew. It swelled until it weighed down my chest. But still I kept my arm over my eyes.

"Huh." Cahir slapped my leg. "You're hungry. Let's go get food."

TEN

Cahir

I KNEW we weren't broken when she took my hand in the supermarket. In that loose, free way she had that didn't require eye contact and happened while she was doing something else like putting her phone in her pocket or pushing her hair one way or the other. I tried not to squeeze her hand too hard. I tried not to think too much, to stay with her, in the moment, to pull her into the moment with me.

She snorted when I said something asinine about lobsters, and I knew she was back. Lobster, scallops, cream, butter, pasta. I threw it in the cart and she stopped me.

"We don't have to." She held the pasta in her hands. "I don't need it."

No. She didn't. She wouldn't. Because she was Cassidy. She was my friend. My best one. And there was a magic in her that did things to me. Excited me, calmed me, healed me.

Loving Zion was lightning and drowning. It was bated breath in dark rooms and twist and turns designed to get you lost and nauseous. I didn't know love before Zion. For a while, I didn't want to know love after her. I wanted to dream of her at night and reach for her in the mornings.

I didn't reach across the bed to pull Zion's body closer to mine anymore though. I reached for my phone to find something to send Cash before she woke in the morning. A funny article or post on social media. A concert I bought us tickets for before she could tell me it wasn't her thing. Craft and art fairs. Thrift stores and swap meets three cities over. Movies. Recipes. Sales on ridiculous things I knew she could make look cool.

But almost every morning there was already something from her waiting for me. A picture of a plant. Coffee. The sunrise. A line from a book she read. A myth about some god or goddess I never heard of.

It was easy with Cash. As easy as waking up in the morning. Fun. Smiles and sunshine and subconscious movements that had no purpose except to pull her closer to me.

Love songs described what I had with Zion. They talked about the torture and the pull. The fire and the way breaks didn't heal even. The obsession to be close. The smell of her in unexpected places. The longing for her that threatened to rip itself out of my chest.

The movies and tv shows said love was misshapen and hard to pass through the reality of an every day life. Love was loud arguments and break ups to make ups and flowers to say sorry or to say nothing at all because she would think what she wanted.

Love wasn't laughter and smiles and the reach across space and time sure that someone would wait for you, want you, on the other end. Love wasn't luxurious. It wasn't a soft place to rest. It didn't make life better or fit into the spaces you made for it. It destroyed.

I couldn't fall for Cash. It would be too much like coming home.

We cooked at my house. Easy and familiar. She picked music I liked. I didn't know when she learned the words. I didn't know when she learned the dances, but I turned down all of the burners on the stove to join her in the living room for a dance break.

She started to cook the pasta but I took it out of her hands and did it myself.

Was that what I wanted? Did I want to have a place in my life that was chaos and an uneven path? Did I want to spend the rest of my life drowning when I could fly? Did I want intensity and anger and fear and disgust and disappointment when there was someone that brought only the best? Only made me better?

I didn't want Zion. The thought shot through me as I brought dinner to the table and imagined the dance Cash would do after her first bite. I almost dropped the bowl. There wasn't supposed to be anything but Zion. There was only supposed to be the misery. There were-

There were just a lot of things I didn't want. And maybe I didn't love Cash yet. Maybe there were a few things to work out. A few hurdles to jump. Maybe.

I ate dinner. I watched her eat and couldn't push the little grin, that little grin that didn't exist before her and couldn't be given to anyone else, off my face.

"Yeah," I said. "I think you're right. I am falling for you."

Her fork clattered to her plate.

∞

Cahir

SHE WENT silent but that was okay. There was as much to hear in her silences as there were in her words. She loaded the dishwasher and wiped down the counters. I made popcorn and poured in M&M's. I picked a movie she liked and laid her favorite pillows on her side of the couch.

She rolled her eyes. I tried to keep the laugh back and failed. We watched the movie with her head in my lap and the popcorn cradled against her stomach. When the movie was over we watched the news and some reality show that made us both shout and groan in disgust.

I fell asleep first. Then her head was on my shoulder, and my sleep got a little better. My phone said it was three in the morning when the empty bowl fell to the ground and woke us.

"I should go." She was almost in my lap. Almost.

"Yeah." My arms tightened around her.

"Okay." She was asleep again.

And so, so light. It was easy to carry her to bed. Easy to lay down beside her and feel her curl into my side and lay her head on my chest. Easy to drift into a sleep that didn't have dreams.

My alarm went off. I turned it off and reached for my phone, ready to find something to text her, something to make her laugh, when I remembered that she was there.

She smiled up at me. "My breath smells disgusting."

So did mine. But I laughed long and loud anyways.

I had a toothbrush for her. She made us eggs. I made toast and poured juice. She got the paper.

"This was lying under the paper," she said.

I didn't like her voice. I didn't like the weight that came into it. I didn't like that the laughter was gone. I didn't like that I wanted to take whatever she held away from her without knowing what it was.

It was a book. A biography.
I didn't like that either.

∞

Cassidy

HE TOLD me to dress like it mattered, like we didn't know each other, like it was something new. Wasn't it, I wanted to ask him. Wasn't it different to wake up beside someone in bed and not have time to prepare, to put on the things that made you feel safe, the armor of fresh clothes and expertly applied make up? Wasn't it different to have only your smile and stale breath and find they were more than enough?

And there was the possibility, the eventuality, of his love. It filled my mind. What would his love look like? What would it feel like? How would it touch me? Did I want to be touched?

I wore leather. That was the armor I chose for the nights that mattered. It slid off my shoulders and draped over my breasts. It clung to my ass and hugged my legs down to my knees.

It was right. I knew it was before I left the house. I knew when I passed through my grandmother's shop and she smiled at me. Proud of me. Proud I came from her.

I knew it was right when I walked into the restaurant and the hostess stopped speaking to the couple in front of me. I knew it was right when I walked through the dark space with its wrought iron railings, round booths and intimate tables, an open dance floor and a man on an acoustic guitar who sang like he wouldn't be satisfied until he broke all of our hearts.

"Holy hell," Cahir said. His fingers brushed my shoulders.

I was shy. I wanted to duck my head in the face of his unabashed admiration. In the face of what he would feel for me if he didn't feel it already. That wasn't how love was supposed to happen, was it? Wasn't it supposed to be equal? What did I do when he crossed into that space? What if I didn't want to follow?

There was pain in that, pain in the possibility of a future without him, without us. I was in leather. I wasn't supposed to feel pain.

I raised my chin. "Yes."

"Cash goddamned money."

There he was. There was my Cahir. I laughed.

"Our table is ready." He put a glass of champagne in my hand. "Are you?"

The restaurant's lights were low. Black tapered candles were on every table, marking the time, building the mood.

Dancing across his skin.

"Yes," I said.

ELEVEN

Cahir

"YOU SAID TABLE AND I THOUGHT," Cash waved her hand, "a table among the rabble. Not this."

I laughed and pushed her chair closer to the table. "The truth is kind of depressing."

"Excellent." She took a sip of her champagne. "Share."

"Zion's here."

"Shit."

I regretted telling her. But I knew I wouldn't be able to lie to her. I knew the truth would make her sympathetic not angry. I knew her.

"Yeah," I said. "Normally I make reservations under my business partners's names or have my assistant do it. But I forgot or I-"

She laid her hand over mine. It was another small table. One for people that wanted to be closer than close but also wanted a place to put their food. The room was large with windows that gifted us with sweeping views of the City as it moved from its day persona to night.

Art and wine covered the walls. Candles filled the empty spaces. And it was cool. A sommelier told me it was to encourage patrons to drink more, eat more, fall in love with spicier food. It just made me want to move closer, to trace my fingers over the goosebumps that rose on Cash's skin.

"And she was here."

"Yeah."

"That's...not normal," she said.

"No." I hadn't thought about it. Nothing between Zion and I had ever been normal.

"How'd you get the room?"

"I dropped O'Shea's name with the manager."

Cash laughed. I thought the candles burned a bit brighter.

"I can't believe that worked," she said.

"It's a give/take kind of thing," I said.

"What do you mean?"

"No menus. Tonight's one of those nights I'm glad I have a little money."

"Why?"

"O'Shea's going to make me pay through the nose for this."

"Does that mean there's going to be a lot of food?"

"Yeah, Cash." I grinned.

She rubbed her hands together. And sat still until my laughter died. "You don't have to lie you know."

"I'd never lie to you." I was rigid in my seat. A little offended. A little angry.

"A little money?" She raised her eyebrow. "I can google your net worth."

"You probably have."

"I have."

I poured her more champagne. "Cash money."

She laughed.

The food came. Course after course. Cash demanded that we pace ourselves. No more than five bites of anything. Every course was boxed and bagged for us to gorge on later. She did well with her rule. Until the porterhouse came in.

"Fuck it." She picked up her fork and knife. "Let's do this."

She rubbed her stomach when there was nothing let on the plate but bone. "You shouldn't have let me do it."

"I wasn't about to get stabbed."

She laughed. "I want to ask you something."

"I want to tell you." And I did.

"There seems to be this kind of pull between you and Zion. We've talked about why you won't go back, but I guess I want to know-"

"Why I won't go back?"

She threw a piece of bread at me. "How you can ignore the draw."

"You know any addicts?"

She shook her head.

"In the tech industry almost everyone's addicted to some shit. They're either about to go to rehab or just got out. Rehab lingo gets folded into ours."

"Okay."

"You learn that an addict will always be an addict. They'll just get better at staying away from the substance. They'll build a life where the substance isn't at the center."

"You'll always love her."

I shrugged. "I'll get real tired of being drawn to something that only wants to hurt and bruise and ruin me."

She nodded, and I wished I could have lied to her.

∞

Cassidy

I CHOSE clothes that didn't cling and didn't drink anything but water. The music was muted and lacked bass. I used my smiles to answer client questions. My words would be too sharp. I was elbows, knees, cheekbones, and squinted eyes.

And I knew why.

I should have felt it coming. I should have predicted it. I should have found a solution.

Kevin and I were...every nasty thought I ever had. We were hot nights and a few moments in the morning where we didn't know if we could look at each other, if the stain of the sins we committed and enjoyed would be visible. We were grasping fingers and screams. Scratched backs and soft caresses. Wet mouth, wet pussy, wet dick. Indecent exposure charges and the gates of heaven.

He banked every fire I tried to set and then set some of his own so I would know what I did was nothing compared to what he was capable of. He was Satan in winter. He was-we were-perfect.

And I left him without having a suitable replacement. I just walked away as if my body would go gently into celibacy and calmly into denial. Nothing felt the same. Nothing. Vibrators agitated. My hands gave me weak orgasms that didn't seem worth the effort when they passed.

I wanted.

I never did well with wanting what I couldn't immediately have.

I slammed things. Things that didn't belong to me. I

yanked clothes onto hangers. I restocked the wine fridge and slammed the door.

"Hey!" Delia's voice ran down the steps. "Fuck up the clothes. Be careful with the rosé."

If it were any other day, if I weren't so on edge, I would have laughed. I wanted to laugh. I couldn't.

I stomped out of the office and up to the third floor as soon as I could without feeling guilty. It was later than I should have stayed. Later than Delia stayed. Later than any of them stayed. My files were organized. My bookmarks were updated with designers to watch and showrooms to contact.

I sighed.

"Can't be that bad."

I sighed again when I heard Cahir's voice. "It is."

"How can I help?"

"You can't."

He sat beside me on the couch and threw an arm over my shoulders. He always smelled so good. Manly. Sea salt, pine, ash, and something I couldn't place. Not that smelling him helped. Not that the way my body turned to his helped. Not that the heat that passed through my body again helped.

"Try me, Cash."

"I said you can't help."

"Whoa." He sounded so amused I wanted to hit him until he was willing to take me seriously. "Now you definitely have to tell me what's wrong."

"Nothing. Really. Nothing."

"You never leave the office this clean. And your laptop is about to die. You hate when that happens."

I did hate that.

"Tell me what's wrong, Cash."

"I'm just feeling irritable today."

"Any reason?"

Oh, I hated his stupid little smirk. "Involuntary celibacy."

"What?"

There it was. The strangled breath. The wide eyes. The open mouth. There.

"You heard me." I could enjoy myself, enjoy his surprise. "Involuntary celibacy makes me irritable."

He looked away from me and rubbed the back of his neck. Then his eyes were on mine and part of me shrank back. Another part considered that it might have been best to keep my thoughts to myself.

"I can help you with that." His voice was deeper than I'd ever heard it.

I blinked. "What?"

TWELVE

Cassidy

HE TURNED ON THE COUCH, knee on the cushions. A barrier? Everything was too hot, too close, too much altogether. The dress that was supposed to be loose and flowy was prison on my skin. I didn't know if I wanted to escape.

"I could help you with that," he said. Again.

Did I look as stupid as I felt, as caught in a trap I didn't know he had the skill to set? Had I ever noticed the intensity he threw like javelins with just his eyes? Had I ever seen his body so still yet so ready? Ready. For what? Was I?

"Be clear, Cahir," I said.

Did I mean that? Did I want clarity? Did I want my clothes? Did I want more of the pounding of my heart and blood and they way they both seemed to race? Did I want to see him, all of him, down to the smallest details and imagine what those details would look like, smell like, taste like, when they mixed with mine?

Did I want to jump?

"Sex. It's been a while for me too. If I'm going to do it

again," his finger trailed a path over my cheek. "I'd like it to be with you."

"Why?"

"Because I'm falling in love with you. Because I think we could burn each other from the inside out. Because I think I can make you forget Kevin existed."

Kevin? I had to think, to breathe, to look away to remember my life before Cahir. Before that moment. Before he touched me for the first time in a way that wasn't just about comfort.

"We probably aren't compatible." I had to say something. Grasp at something. Ignore the way my body disagreed with me and wanted me to defile that couch, him.

"Cash." That finger trailed over my shoulder. I wished it were bare. "You don't have to tell lies."

"I have to do something."

"Touch yourself."

"What?"

"You heard me." He pulled all of the air in the room to him.

"I can't-"

"You can. You'll have more fun if you do." He grinned.

I thought I knew all of his grins. That one was new. Wicked. And I was weak.

My fingers skimmed over the places he already touched. My cheeks. My shoulders. The straps of my dress fell and trapped my arms. I looked at him. It was more than I was ready for-this loosening of my armor. I needed him.

"Touch and tell?" The grin was still on his face. One eye brow lifted.

"Cahir."

"Touch yourself and tell me how you'd like it to be."

Was this us? Was this what was below the surface of the

smiles and the jokes and holding hands at the farmer's market? Was that heat always there, waiting for me, when we watched movies or wandered through a museum?

"Tell me what you like, Cash."

I cleared my throat. Again. And pushed the straps, the top of my dress, down to pool around my belly button. I was a B cup on my best day. A modest handful. Cahir's eyes ran over me, and I felt like more than enough.

"I like when it's soft at first. Easy. I like learning and teasing." My hands skimmed the roundness of the bottoms of my breasts. Up. Over. Down. Down to circle my nipples. Slow circles that moved inward and seemed to hypnotize him.

"I like when it feels like passion may kill us but it won't kill time. We have so much time to die." My fingers brushed over my nipples. No. I wouldn't close my eyes. I would see him. I would see myself. "I like kisses that go on forever. They change but don't end. Simple to rough to quick so we can breathe. I like to feel your tongue. I like to find the places where you hide all of the tastes. I like skin. Under my lips. Under my fingers. I like when-"

He stood and slipped out of his jacket. It was tossed over the back of the couch. So was his tie. "Keep going."

"I like the way you sound."

He unbuttoned his shirt and sat down. He put one of my hands on his chest and dragged it down to his waist. And he leaned close and moaned low and soft and fast. Fast enough that the sound could have belonged to my imagination instead of him.

"Like that?"

I nodded.

"Words, Cash."

Who was he? Why hadn't I tried to meet him sooner?

I ran my nose up the shell of his ear. He moaned again. He was warm. His body and smell. I wanted to be closer. Closer. I moved. My leg curled behind his back. My dress just a sash around my waist.

"Let me help."

My pretty French panties became a belt of torn rags around my waist. My body a pillar of feeling waiting and hoping for him to do more. To take us too far. To ruin my clothes, my hair, my make up, my life. Ruin. Ruin. Collapse. Take.

"Please, Cahir."

He didn't moan. His forehead rested on my shoulder to watch my fingers find the place that needed my attention most. To see those fingers flutter and tease. Collect and spread the wetness he brought to the surface. I watched and tried to see what he saw, but I could barely see at all. There was only what I felt. Him. His breath whispered over my breasts. His shirt teased my thighs. His legs pushed me wider when he moved.

The lowering of his zipper was like an explosion. "Tell me if it's too much. Tell me if it's too far."

"I want to see." I licked my lips. Dry lips. Dry mouth. Empty mind.

Empty and my God, he was beautiful. I shouldn't have been surprised. Long. Thick. Dripping. Leaking. Oh.

"And I want to hear, Cash."

"Cahir."

"I'm going to make you say that word a lot."

I smiled. He wouldn't have to make me do anything. The way he touched himself. Strong, sure. Rough then loose. Demanding then unfocused.

"Tell me," I said.

Maybe I begged. Maybe he heard the desperation.

Maybe he knew me and that was why we were in that situation in the first place. He saw what I wouldn't say.

"I want to see you on your knees. Your eyes open wide but not as wide as your mouth. I want to see your hands drag up my legs. I want to see your nails dig into me when I give you a bit more than you thought I had."

I would die. From the words alone. A glorious death. Oh.

"You'll look at me and I'll know you like the taste, the moment. I'll tell you what a good girl you are and tell you what I want next."

My fingers slipped through my wetness, slipped inside me. "What do you want next?"

"Good girl." His lips dragged over my jaw.

Oh, God. Oh.

"I'll want you to lay on your back. I'll want you to pull your knees up. Up to your ears so I can see all of you. And I'm going to want you to stay like that when I put my mouth on you. Perfectly still. If you aren't, I'll hit you here." He ran a nail over the inside of my thighs.

The thought of him hitting me shouldn't have made my breath tangle in my throat, but it did. I knew I would pass out. "You want to hurt me?"

Nose to nose. Eye to eye. Mouths opened, but they didn't touch. Not once.

"I want to give orders. I want them to be obeyed. I want to reward your obedience."

There. Shit, fuck, goddamn, there. It was a dark, roaring place that I toppled into. One that shook me and wrenched a shriek out of me when it refused to release me.

I was curled up in a corner of the couch when my brain, my body, decided they were mine again. My dress was right. My panties gone.

And he stood in the twilight shadows and made his clothes right again. I knew him. Knew him well. It shouldn't have touched me that he saw to me first.

He smiled and pulled me up to him. Arms tight around me. If I thought it was a dream, a hallucination, the bulge that pressed into my stomach told me otherwise and made my body tight again.

He laughed into my ear. Was that who he'd been all along? A man who could laugh like that? A man that could take the strength out of my legs.

He kissed the top of my head. "Soon."

THIRTEEN

Cassidy

I BREEZED into my grandmother's shop and scooped things into the basket I normally reserved for the farmer's market. Oils, incense, crystals, candles. I put money on the counter and smiled at her.

"I tell you not to leave this mess here." The disgust in her voice wasn't real. The smile on her face was.

"Money is never mess, Gran."

"And your money is never any good here." She always wore white. Billowing white. It moved around her when she leaned over the counter to see what was in my basket. Her eyes went wide. "Oh, really?"

And perhaps I did look like the cat that ate all of the canaries but that was no one's business but mine.

"Really."

"Well." She swept from behind the counter and looped her arm through mine. "It's been slow today. I can watch you prepare your home for a nice bit of nasty sex."

I laughed. "Junie's coming over too."

"Good. I haven't seen that girl in so long."

Junie leaned against my door, attention on her nails until she saw my grandmother. I was shoved away. "Auntie May."

Gran was Auntie May to everyone. The woman with the sight and the truth. The one with the healing you needed. She was the reason I could run through Strawberry Fields without a care in the world. She was sacred to them. To me she was just Gran.

"Did she tell you?" Junie followed me into my apartment and moved to my kitchen.

"Don't drink all of my wine, June," I said.

"I brought my own. Think I'm a fucking amateur?"

Gran and I smiled at each other. I swept and mopped. Threw open all of my windows and watered my plants. I turned on music that made my hips move in slow circles meant to endure. I lit the incense and held each of the candles. Emptied myself and filled them.

"I watch her and I'm always so proud," Gran said.

"I've never done all this to fuck someone. Am I missing out?" Junie's gum was raspberry. A good smell.

I held out my hand for a piece. She rolled her eyes.

"Share, Junie," Gran said.

Junie stopped mid-eye roll and slapped a piece of gum in my hands.

"It depends," I said when the taste of raspberry and sugar and summer sweet filled my mouth. "Did you know it was coming?"

"I better be coming. Only reason I show up."

Gran snickered. Gray twists swinging over her shoulders and down her back.

"Junie," I said.

She took a sip of wine. A deep rosé. Looked good. I poured glasses for me and Gran.

"You mean was it premeditated and shit?" Junie stared into her wine. "Nah. Spontaneous. It's easier that way."

My mouth was open. Mind filled with questions. Gran shook her head. I swallowed them back.

"It's like anything else in life. The better the energy is, the better the experience is. I'm just doing the early work to make sure my energy, my home's energy, is right."

"For Cahir?"

I shrugged. "And for me."

"I've never wanted to do all this for a man," Junie settled deeper into my sofa.

"Most of them don't deserve it," Gran said. "But when it's a friend..."

"I've been saying they should get to fucking for a while now," Junie said.

Gran hooted.

"But now that it's happening it's a little weird. Like a little. Cause they're friends."

I stopped sorting through the clutter on my tv console. "Isn't it better when you're friends? That first time is always so awkward and weird. But this is someone that knows you. That likes you for just you and has shown you over and over. You've given them secrets and memories. They give you the same. There's already intimacy. Why not a bit more?"

"Is that what you're hoping to get? A bit more?"

I slid a glance to Junie. "Sister-friend, I'm planning on getting a whole lot more."

She snorted into her wine.

∞

Cassidy

HIS EYES RAN OVER ME, what was illuminated by the candle light. "So we're not watching a movie tonight. For sure."

I laughed and pulled him into my apartment. I skimmed a hand over the sheer robe that covered the bra that barely covered anything with its mesh panel and appliqué and the panties that served no other purpose than to match my bra.

"You look beautiful," he said.

I felt it. Gran braided my hair into a crown after she oiled it. I put flower petals and gently scented oils into my bath. I lit my candles and danced through my own shadows. I felt beautiful. And strong.

And he looked like a man. Casual and easy. Relaxed and open. Ready. Whenever I was.

"Do you want wine?"

He smiled. The same smile from the Lonely Third. My body had the same reaction.

"I haven't been thinking about wine all day, Cash."

"No?"

Our feet moved down the hall through the living room. His clothes were quieter than whispers when they drifted to the floor. Or perhaps it was that the beating of my heart was so loud I couldn't hear anything else. Was that what anticipation was? The tingling of fingers and toes? The adrenaline that raced through the body? The bending of time so each step felt like an eternity and nothing all at once?

Dozens of candles lit the bedroom. Warmed it. They smelled like my favorite plants, flowers, herbs, and woods.

Woods. It smelled like I was about to lay down in the forest and let Cahir make love to me.

I turned to face him. Tears almost sprang to my eyes. His naked body was...

Perfection.

His steps were slow. As if I would grow wings and fly away.

"I won't run," I said. "I want to be close too."

He smiled. One of the smiles I knew before our time on the couch. "You always know."

"I'm your friend."

His hands cupped my cheeks. "My best one."

Then he kissed me. And we didn't fit. A meeting of lips and minds that should have made perfect sense. But the timing. I was fast when he was slow. He was insistent when I retreated. I was rough when he was gentle. We pulled away. I wasn't disappointed. Surprised maybe. After the other day, I just knew. I was so sure.

"Did you like it when you did it your way?" There was another of the grins I didn't know. I had never heard his voice so raw.

I shook my head.

"My turn?"

I shrugged. We could laugh about it. No matter what we would be friends and we could laugh about it. He would still hold my hand and play in my hair.

"Okay."

One of his hands hooked behind my neck and pulled. Oh. Another lay flat on my stomach and pushed. I would have tripped into him if he weren't so sure.

He didn't kiss me so much as sip from me as those hands ran wild over my body. Little tugs and pecks. Brief explorations as his hands set me on fire.

I gasped.

I felt and heard how that pleased him.

He dove. He pulled me under with him.

It wasn't a kiss. It was drowning and falling from the highest place. It was nausea and dizziness and craving. Craving more. If it ended I would die.

He pushed the flimsy robe off my shoulders. My panties and bra fell away. There were just his hands.

I had hands. Yes. I ran them over him. I let them fall into the ridges his abs made and into the lines that cut across his thighs and promised he would be able to give me what I wanted most. I dipped into the place where muscles gave way to his spine.

And I thought I would spend an eternity dying. He made me feel like there was no time. There was just what we did. What he did. I could only hang onto him. Reach for him and find him when it felt like too much.

I whimpered into his mouth, and he laid us on my bed. The sheets were softer than I imagined. The bed larger and smaller. I smelled everything. Him. Had I ever smelled anything before him?

I buried my nose in his neck then ran it down his body. Mine. He smelled like mine. And that was fine for the moment. I would let that feeling live in the moment. There would be time to think about the past and the future later.

But there was one thing, a memory from the not so distant past that stayed with me. I wanted to see.

I pulled him up from the bed. He kissed me and I let him. I gave myself to it. Until my head began to swim and I almost forgot. Then I fell to my knees. I tilted my head back. And I opened my mouth.

"My God." He touched my cheeks. "You're going to kill me."

He tasted like fall. Crisp and a little warm and unfamiliar after a long summer of heated breezes. He was loud like the wind when it picked up all of a tree's leaves. Fierce as the strong winds that brought tears to your eyes.

And he did bring tears to my eyes. There was so much of him. My mouth burned as it stretched around him. And it was so good. So right. My hands were as busy as my mouth. They ran over me. Sank into me. Made me dizzy and motivated.

I came when he did and marveled at the symmetry. At the way he stayed hard in my mouth.

"Did you swallow it all?"

His tongue was in my mouth before I could answer. Disgusting. He was absolutely disgusting, and I couldn't wait for him to give me more. Show me how much deeper into the filth and societally unacceptable he could go.

Back on the bed. My knees kissing my ears. I smiled at him. Maybe my smile was new because he froze, blinked.

"Fucking hell." And he was on me.

I didn't have bones. It was the only way my back could arch like that. No spine. No ribs. I could shrink, arch, collapse, and melt. I was new.

I was in the dark. A room full of candles and he gave me a pleasure that made me blind. Oh.

Fuck.

The first orgasm put cramps in my feet. My calves. The second ripped my voice out of my body. The third made me cry. The fourth made me forget. Like he said it would. And like he said, his name dripped from my lips and slid down my body to his ears, to the mouth that moaned over the taste of me.

Somehow I knew better than to push him away. Knew it would be better if I just endured.

The fifth orgasm made my body flutter. Like a butterfly. Soft little undulations that didn't stop when he crawled up my body and kissed me until everything tasted and smelled like me.

"We're not done," he whispered in my ear.

FOURTEEN

Cahir

I THOUGHT all I would ever want to do in my life was drown. Then Cassidy. Cash. I touched her and knew what it was to fly home. Everything about her was familiar and wanted. I yearned for it. Reached further for it.

I didn't know what made me open my mouth that day on the couch. I projected bravado and choked on my fear. Shit. It was right there. But she let me pick up the possibility and see where it led.

Her body was magic. Like the rest of her. There was no surprise in that. Just caution. To do it all right. To give her what she deserved.

Had my name ever sounded so good? Had a woman ever tasted-And when she got on her knees...

I'd had women lose their good sense for me. Ready to twist themselves into whatever odd shape they thought a rich man wanted. Whatever shape would make me call them again. I never called. They were all the same.

Cash was burned on my brain. Burned through my

lungs. Lit my appetite. I gorged on her and still there wasn't enough. Still, I felt so free. Every second I spent touching her was a second I felt more like myself. The self I wanted to be but didn't think I would ever get to. It was right there. The map to my best self was etched into her skin. I only had to please her to get it.

I said I wouldn't worship a woman again. It was danger-ous. I wouldn't survive. But I hadn't had Cash. I hadn't had a woman that would worship me back. Every time she said my name it was both a prayer and a hallelujah. And it spurred me.

I liked the way her body broke for me. I liked that when it was broken it still felt indestructible. I liked the feeling of power in my hands. I knew how easily she could take it away.

I kissed her. Kissed her until we both tasted the same and then I slid my fingers back inside her.

Slow, slow. Easy. I wanted my fingers to play like her imagination did. I wanted to see her lose her mind.

The flush creeped up her body. The tears fell down. Her chest rose high with each breath.

"Gorgeous," I said.

Every part of her body pressed and shuddered against mine when she came. Soft as spring.

Her eyes were wide. Not with surprise. The part of me that was sometimes too close to being a caveman swelled with pride at that. That she knew. She knew what I would be. What I could do.

She jerked her chin to her nightstand. I reached in the drawer. Condoms. I sat up. Held them. Stared at them. Hated myself for bringing memories of her into the room with Cash and I.

"I bought them today. And I didn't open the box. The

receipt's in the drawer too." Her voice was quiet. Understanding. Too compassionate for what I deserved.

The box was still shrink-wrapped. Safe. I looked down at her. My friend. My best one. The one that knew and just wanted me to feel safe.

She failed.

I didn't feel safe. I felt dangerous. I wanted to tear her apart.

The onslaught began slowly. A slow push of my body into hers. She was wet. So wet. And still there resistance. So I put my mouth on her and made her scream my name. And while she buzzed from what my mouth made her feel, I slid into her again. Halfway. She panted. Tightened and released around me.

"There's more."

"Oh, my God."

"Yeah. I could be." I pressed deeper into her.

She pulled her legs back.

My eyes rolled until everything was dark. For a moment. Just a moment. I sank deeper into her. I didn't want her to end.

But I found the end of her. She wrapped her arms around my neck. I kissed her. The long kisses that told her to relax. She would want to relax. She did. And I pushed deeper inside her.

I liked her gasp. The shock in it. The dirtiness in it. There were so many ways I could make her dirty.

Just hips. To begin I used just my hips to grind into her. Until she rocked to meet me. Then more. A bit more until she opened her eyes wide and fell open. Open like the flowers she loved. Body loose.

Hand under her ass. I gripped her. I fucked her. I made love to her.

I found a piece of myself I didn't know I needed.

I told her to come and she obeyed me. I fell into her. I exploded. Imploded. Simply ceased to exist.

Cash.

Cassidy.

Witch.

I didn't check the condom for holes when I took it off. I only wanted it off. I only wanted to put on another and be inside her again.

FIFTEEN

Cahir

SHE WAS THERE in the morning. Body sprawled over mine. Mouth everywhere. Everywhere. I moaned before I opened my eyes. I moaned when I opened them.

Want looked like a satin bonnet dangerously close to falling off. Like limbs reaching long to find the place that had been hidden before. Want looked like mouth on skin. Pulling skin. Biting and soothing at once. Want was bright, brown eyes on mine. Want was the smile in them. The concentration.

I gave into it. Gave into her.

I opened the condom. She rolled it on. Then she was there. And God. Oh, God. Fucking God. Fucking hell.

If she would just. For a moment. Just-Not slower. Not-no. I wouldn't deny myself that kind of-Shit. Fingers dug into flesh. Hers into mine. Mine into hers. Maybe I hurt her. Maybe she hurt me. Maybe we bled into her sheets or maybe everything was okay.

How could anything be okay when she could make her body do that to mine?

She smiled. She smiled when she rode me. Bit her lip. In the moments I could keep my eyes open, I saw that.

Head by mine. Hair everywhere. It smelled like lavender and made me want her more. I would explode. Her mouth by my ear. Open. Not to give me words. To let me hear what her pleasure sounded like.

And control. I knew control. Held it in my hands. Owned it. With everyone. Everyone but her.

I gave her what she wanted, and she smiled at me in the light of the early morning sun. Reds and pinks and a touch of orange.

The sound of wet condom when it hits the floor and then her mouth-All the way back. To the back of her throat it felt like. And I found I had more to give.

We showered together. We found other uses for her kitchen counter. Her wall. My secretary called about the meeting I was a little too close to being late for. I couldn't answer her. My mouth was busy with...other things.

And found those things again at lunch. In my office.

At dinner in her home.

The next day in mine.

And so the pattern became new again. But the same. Because at the center was Cash. Always at the center. And there, in the moments we gave each other to breathe, to tremble, to laugh, incredulous, at the universe for our good fortune, was my friend. My best one.

∞

Cassidy

"LET'S GO," he said.

He wore the smile I'd known longer and liked better since seeing the other smiles he had, the faces that passion made him make. And I didn't recognize myself. But I said what we both knew I would.

"Yes."

I packed a bag and met him at the airfield where the private jet he rented idled on the tarmac. He took my hand. When the plane reached cruising altitude, he took my body. Again and again.

We spent the weekend in Philly in dinky buildings that housed beautiful restaurants. At a music festival where I snapped photo after photo not of the artists but of their fans and the outfits they wore. In a private cigar bar with more whiskey than I'd ever seen.

We walked and held hands and kissed wherever we felt like because we hadn't told anyone there that we were just friends.

Not that we were anything besides friends.

He took me shopping. I didn't mean for him to. I walked into an interesting looking boutique and touched things, liked some things, and fell in love with others.

He rolled his eyes at the register when his credit card came out before mine, when I protested. "Shut up, Cash."

He sounded so much like my friend, just my friend, that I did.

We went to a farmer's market because we both admitted the weekend didn't feel like the weekend without it. We ate fruit from our perch on the sidewalk until the juices of it ran down our arms.

We went back to the hotel room and cleaned each other off.

And then we were back on the plane. Sweat-slicked

bodies pressed close together, the after swells of the magic we made every time we touched made our fingers, arms, feet, toes, touch. Made us smile.

And "us" became something new. A thing that I couldn't put my finger on or give a name to. "Us" swelled and filled and turned and twisted into shapes I never saw before. The places it filled were unfamiliar to me. Places that I didn't know were lacking. Places that I didn't know were waiting for him.

I rested my head on his shoulder. It didn't matter. None of it mattered. Except that he was just my friend. My best one.

∞

Cahir

I DIDN'T HOLD her hand when we were back in the City and didn't know why. No. That wasn't entirely true. I still held her hand. But I didn't kiss her fingers. I didn't pull her close to make kissing her lips easier. My hand didn't flirt with her waist or slip into her back pocket. It didn't wrap around the back of her neck to feel her shiver.

Sometimes she moved closer to me. A sway of the body. Raised eyes full of an expectation I didn't think she realized she carried. A smile she didn't realize curved her lips. Sometimes she reached for me. Sometimes the fingers that were raised to lips were mine. Sometimes the words died on her lips and then her clothes were gone.

I wished I could say dramatic things like my body burned for her. Or that I'd been struck by lightening. But no. What I felt for Cash was a low, quiet hunger. The hunger that comes when you know that you have exactly what you want to eat within arms reach. The kind of hunger that you want to enjoy before you sate it because it reminds you of exactly how alive you are.

We didn't have a reason to be out in public. I didn't want to be. I knew she didn't want to be either. It was just a game we played. How long could we last? Where would we lose it? Who would be the one to give the touch that made not being connected unbearable?

It made us walk. From my apartment to the street full of coffee shops, restaurants, a sex shop. We saw it at the same time and grinned. I took her hand and led her across the street to it. I would have opened the door for her if it hadn't swung open. So fast and strong I pulled her back, behind me.

I looked her over to make sure she was okay. She smiled at me. Then she smiled at him.

"Kevin."

He held the hand of a small woman. The woman held a bulging bag and wore a smile of her own. One of those open happy smiles that's almost always inappropriate for the situation it's used in.

"Cassidy."

I didn't like the longing that passed over his face. I didn't like the way he said her name.

Her hand slid into mine. "Have a good day."

Her voice was polite, neutral. His face was confused. The woman whose hand he held lost her smile.

And Kevin just stood in the doorway.

"Champ," I said. "Can we get past you?"

"Oh." He moved a little. Into the store instead of out of it. "Cassidy we should catch up soon."

"No. I don't think we should." Words for him. Eyes on mine.

I was going to have to fuck her. Soon.

We moved deeper into the store. When I looked away from Cash, Kevin was gone.

"I haven't spoken to him. Or called him or anything," Cash said.

"Was that his wife?"

She laughed. "No."

That laugh. That genuine, easy laugh. I felt my heart flip, turn, swell, twist, become something new. Something that made me pull in a little too much air a little too sharply. And then I settled.

"Cahir."

I looked down at her. The same. Exactly the same and yet completely different. No, I was different. Holy hell. I was brand new.

"I haven't been in contact with him."

"I believe you."

"I just didn't want you to think that I wouldn't consider your feelings-"

Oh. Of course. I saw her. I saw what she felt. Why hadn't I seen that sooner?

"Cash, why are you so worried about this?"

I watched her turn the question over in her mind. I watched her eyes widen.

I smiled at her. "Yeah. I think so too. Do you need to go home?"

She nodded. I wanted to laugh, but I knew how she would react.

I took her home.

SIXTEEN

Cassidy

IT WAS SUPPOSED to be a good day. It was supposed to be a phenomenal day. I was supposed to buy sex toys I didn't need. Cahir was going to take my clothes off. Every time he took my clothes off he looked at me like he'd never seen me before and couldn't believe his good fortune. I was going to spread my legs wide and sigh at the first flicker of his tongue over my pussy. It was always light, that first moment. It was always more than I prepared for.

I was going to make a mess of someone's sheets, someone's home. I was going to sweat and feel his, luxuriate in it. I was going to smell all the new smells desire brought to rest on his skin. I was going to hear him call for me, beg for me, grunt, groan, moan. I was going to have him.

But fucking Kevin.

Kevin just had to ruin it all. Oh, he just had to show me how over him I was. Wasn't I happy living in the world I built? The bubble I built?

I saw him and saw a man. Not the day I met him. Our

day. Not dancing in the dark. Not sex in the wildest of places. Not the exhaustion. I saw a man holding the hand of a woman that wasn't his wife. And I felt sadness for her. Her and the wife. Worry for Cahir. I didn't want him to think for a moment that he wasn't enough, that there was a thought in my mind for Kevin. There wasn't.

There was just Cahir. And I wouldn't hurt him. I wouldn't betray him. I wouldn't take his trust and devalue it. The idea of it, the thought-it crumpled me. It hurt me. Not Cahir. I would hurt myself before I hurt Cahir.

I didn't know how to say it. But I wanted him to know. I wanted him to see that I would bleed before he would. I would fight before he saw the threat. I would-

And then he looked at me and smiled. I saw what he saw. I saw myself. And I knew.

I knew. He knew. And I had to get out. Go. Be alone. He saw that too. He took me home and didn't touch me. He didn't say a word. He knew me so well he didn't even turn on music. He didn't kiss me when he walked me to my door. He only smiled. That smile. I almost slapped it off his face. Punched it off.

But no. I worked hard to control my temper. I worked hard to walk in love and light.

I sat in my house. With my plants. My babies. I thought I would crawl out of my own goddamned skin.

I watered them. I swept and mopped. I cleaned my windows. With newspaper and vinegar. I washed my sheets. I reorganized my closet. I laid on those freshly cleaned sheets that still smelled like sex. I washed them again.

I made taco salad. If Cahir were there he would have run to the store for nacho cheese Doritos. I would have laughed at his disgusting American habits and-But I wasn't supposed to think about Cahir. Not when I still wanted to slap the grin off his face.

Because he knew. Fuck him though.

I meditated. Or tried to. When it failed I turned on my playlist of soothing rain noises. But they only agitated me.

It was midnight and I laid out across my hardwood floors. My hair was a ball of tangled frizz. My socks didn't match. They always matched. And I promised to always be honest with myself. Not because it was a better way to live but because I learned when I was young that I was shit at running away from the truth.

I sat up. I wanted to sleep, and I knew it wouldn't happen until I spoke the truth.

"I'm falling in love with Cahir," I said to the ancestors, the air, my plants, myself. "Fuck."

∞

Cassidy

HE WAS NOT the best choice. He was not a choice at all. A man in love with his ex. A man who would have to share his affections, his heart. A man that couldn't come to me whole because pieces of him were with another. Sure, he was different from the man I met. Sure, he laughed more, smiled more. Sure, it had been weeks since I saw the shadows pass over his face. And we didn't talk about the past anymore. Zion and Kevin weren't interesting topics of conversation.

There was never a moment I felt like his body was with me while his mind was with her. There was never a moment that I didn't feel like the center.

But still. There had to be boundaries. There had to be

rules. There had to be a way to control or curb what was happening.

I thought it over at work. Over and over and over. While the music was loud and the camera was pressed to my face as I photographed clients for their social media and mine. While I popped bottles of champagne and talked to them about their vacations, their lovers, their dreams. While I made them smile and reminded them why they followed me from The Agency to Beyond.

When it was over, Cahir was there. I knew before I turned. Knew by the way my last clients acted. A group of girls that couldn't come see me alone. They got it in their heads that they were going to be the new New Money Girls. I didn't have the time to explain to them why that was a futile idea. I just took their money and gave them clothes. They tittered. They preened.

"Cahir, go talk to Junie," I said.

I heard his laughter trail down the hall, down the steps.

He was back twenty minutes later. I was on the couch.

"Rough day?" He slipped my heels off my feet and massaged my instep.

"You can't do that."

"Why not? Got other plans for us?"

I would have laughed. If I didn't know what I knew, I would have laughed. "We have to talk."

"If you were anyone else, I would be worried."

"I think what we're doing needs some parameters."

"It doesn't, but I'm willing to listen."

"Cahir, be serious."

"I am." He pressed his thumbs in just above the heel of my foot. I thought I would die.

"You aren't."

"Need me to bleed on the floor, Cash?"

Was I supposed to tell him I could find better uses for his blood? Would that freak him out?

"I don't like the look in your eye."

I laughed and that felt like betrayal. "Friends with benefits."

"No."

"You didn't even let me finish." I tugged my feet out of his grasp.

"I don't need to hear a whole lot of words to recognize a bad idea."

It was the grin on his face that wiped the laughter and joy off of mine. I wanted to protect myself. I wanted to be safe. I wanted to avoid nights in my bed without him. I wanted to avoid longing and jealousy and pain. What if we couldn't handle it?

"We need boundaries."

"What are you afraid of?"

My insides churned. "Fuck you, Cahir."

Someone, sometime, might have taught me that anger was not the best reaction, that it accomplished nothing. But how else would I protect myself when I was afraid? How else would I explain the way my hands shook? Better to let the heat rise in me than succumb to the numbness of vulnerability.

"I will. But I don't think that'll really fix the problem."

I hated him. "Friends with benefits. It'll help me deal with the fact that I'm only going to get half a man at best."

"Half?"

There should have been some triumph in the way his brows rose and his voice dropped. "You're in love with someone else."

"I'm in love with you."

Matter of fact. Humble. Soft. I couldn't swallow his

words. So I let my hand swing forward and tightened in anticipation at the feel of my palm cracking across his face.

Instead his hand manacled around my wrist. I was yanked off of the couch. Our height difference never mattered until that moment when I realized my feet dangled and strained to reach the floor.

He laughed before he kissed me. Ugly and cruel, I wished he'd hissed at me instead. I wished the fight, the way I twisted my body and pulled my mouth from his to gulp down air were all real.

"Do you want to fight, little Cash?" A hand around my wrist. Another around my neck.

Was this fighting? Was the way I went wet and soft for him proof that I wanted more?

No. I had to protect myself. I had to show him that I wasn't someone to laugh at. And I wasn't weak.

I kicked out and that leg was wrapped around his waist. I tried with the other leg and found myself locked against him.

Mannequins crashed to the ground. The soft tinkle and slide of jewelry as it fell to the floor. It hurt when my head crashed against the glass. At least I thought it was my head. I thought it hurt. His hand was in my hair-pulling. When I gasped his mouth was there. When I went limp his body held me up.

"Tell me you don't want it."

I fumbled for his pants, his belt.

"Not the sex."

I stared into warm brown eyes that weren't going to back down and walk away. Brown eyes that got closer to mine. His forehead rested on mine. His lashes tickled mine.

"Say you want it, Cash." His fingers caught my chin before I could turn away.

And he stood. With my body pinned against the glass wall that looked into what was once Zion's office. His eyes never left mine.

The trembling started in my hands and moved up until I had to bite my lip. Not that that stopped the tears. He kissed away as many as he could catch.

"I want it," I whispered.

His zipper was loud when he yanked it down.

SEVENTEEN

Cahir

MY NOSE WAS full of her. My back burned where she scratched me. My ears rang with her screams. Shit, my ears rang with my own shouts. My legs burned from the effort. My arms, too.

I was alive.

Smiling. Cash made me smile. When she brought me breakfast that morning in bed then straddled my face and gave me something else to eat. When she fixed my tie. Not because she wanted to touch me. She did that the entire time we got dressed. When I pulled clothes off hangers and when she realized I unpacked her bag while she slept. Her toothbrush was cozier, happier, next to mine, I said. She laughed and kissed my shoulder.

She dropped me off at work. Her fingers pressed into the parts of me that burned until all of me was on fire for her and I dragged her across the seat to straddle me. The windows fogged. Maybe the car rocked. Or maybe I only thought that as a way to explain what happened to me.

I smiled in the elevator at my staff. They went silent. Had it been that long since I smiled? I laughed at them and talked about nothing until their shoulders relaxed and I felt like more of an asshole. I used to have easy relationships with them. We used to have beer and tacos delivered to the office because none of us wanted to go home even though there was no more work to do. We went on company trips.

All that stopped with Zion.

Idiot. It didn't have to be that way.

Not that I knew that until Cash. When I was with her, I was just with her. I didn't become her. I wasn't absorbed into her moods, her wants, her demands. I didn't drown. I was me. And whenever I wanted, I could fly. She would be beside me. To keep me away from the sun. To urge me to do something reckless. Whenever I wanted, I could leave. I was a part of her life not her whole life. She didn't need me to complete her.

I thought that would hurt. To not be the center of someone's world, their focus. It was relieving. Empowering. It calmed me. Focused me. Made me more ambitious. Just made me more. I was proud of that.

"Cahir."

The way my assistant, Melody, said my name made me stop in my tracks. I had to push my shoulders down, stop the tremble in my hands.

"Okay," I said.

I pushed open the door to my office. Clean. Everything clean, modern. When it didn't smell like a funeral home, it was one of my favorite places to be.

There had to be four dozen flowers in the vase. Red and dark crimson roses. Anemones. Aster. Pink Camellia. Lilies. Red and pink carnations. White clover.

I wouldn't have been able to name them without Cash

and our weekly trips to the farmer's market. If the first time I bought her a bucket of flowers she hadn't carefully picked out certain ones and told me what they symbolized and why they weren't welcome in her home.

Zion sent me a big bouquet of "this love just won't die".

"Melody."

The door was too thick for her to hear me, but Melody always knew.

"Yeah, Cahir." She had a broom in her hand.

And I remembered that the last time Zion sent me flowers I let them sit. Through most of the day. I didn't know what I was trying to prove. Then, in the middle of a meeting with Colton, I shoved them off my desk. I didn't like the way Colton kept talking as if my shitty behavior should be ignored. I didn't like the quick flash of sympathy and understanding that crossed his face. I didn't like that Melody was there to clean up after me. I hated it. I hated it all.

I picked up the vase. She took a deep breath. I hated that too.

"Do something with these, please?" I handed them to her.

"Throw them away, you mean." She wrinkled her nose. "They smell like dead people."

I laughed. "No. Just get them out of here."

She didn't look at me like I was crazy even though that was how I felt. It was smarter to throw them away. It was what I should have suggested.

∞

Cassidy

"I'VE BEEN THINKING," I said.

Dinner was over. Everything cleaned and put away. We sprawled across his couch with wine in our hands and lamplight on our faces.

"God." He rolled his eyes and grimaced. "I hate when you women do that."

I laughed so hard he had to take the wine out of my hand. "I've been thinking."

"What have you been thinking, Cash?"

"About how you can be in love with Zion and me."

I did think about it. A lot. And if he were any other man, I wouldn't have asked. I wouldn't have been able to handle tense bodies, anger, impatience that I would bring up a woman I'd never seen when we were so happy. I wouldn't have been able to remain calm when I was called insecure or told that I was harping on something that didn't even matter.

But he wasn't any other man. He was Cahir. He wasn't tense. He handed me my wine and settled deeper into the couch with his own.

"I think it's a two part thing," he said.

I could see him roll and examine the words in his head before they came out of his mouth. Kevin did something like that, and it always set me on edge even though I couldn't figure out why at the time. Cahir just wanted to get it right.

"Okay."

"The two of you are nothing alike. Absolutely nothing." He chuckled. "And I'm grateful for that. I couldn't survive Zion twice, and I can't imagine a life that doesn't have you in it. Us."

Us. I was too smart to react to that one.

"There was so much wrong with me. So much wrong with her. Too much wrong with us even though I couldn't see that at the time. Love isn't supposed to throw your whole life off track. Love isn't obsession. Love isn't walking around all the time feeling like you're drowning or can't breathe. That's drama. Who wants that all the time? Who can sustain that all the time?"

"Huh."

He laughed. "Being with her was-I remember after she left the first time, I told myself I would rather be miserable with her than smiling with someone else. I was proud of that. I thought it was so fucking romantic. I thought it said so much about my devotion to her. I thought it was justification to chase down a woman that couldn't talk to me when things went wrong. Just talk. Even though she said she loved me."

I took away his wine glass and let him squeeze my hand instead.

"Instead it proved I was an idiot. Who decides that love should make them miserable or justify being miserable? How low have you sunk that misery is what you look for and you're willing to abandon joy? Miserable? No. Fuck that. I want to smile. Every day for the rest of my life. I don't want to live in misery." He looked down at my hand. And blinked. Looked around for his wine. "Sorry."

"Don't apologize for something I did." I gave him his wine.

"You two aren't alike. I'm not walking around with the exact same kind of love for two identical women. The way I feel about you is yours. Just yours. No one's had it before you. No one will get it if you decide to leave."

It wasn't the wine that made my body warm and reality loose. "What's the second part?"

"There's a part of me that loves Zion. All of me knows I can't be with her. Every single fiber of my being knows what

I'd be signing up for if I went back to her." He shrugged. "So yeah. I love her. But that doesn't mean anything. It doesn't influence any of my decisions."

"What if-"

"I hate this game."

When he rolled his eyes that time I knew he meant it. I wished I had something small to throw at him. "What if she fixed it all? What if she went to therapy and realized the error of her ways and got all of her shit together? What if it were obvious that she got it all together? Would you go back to her?"

"I don't live in the world of 'what if'. Either it happened or it didn't."

"Cahir."

"Cash."

"Don't."

He took a deep breath. "I don't know. I haven't thought about it. I don't want to think about it. It's a colossal waste of my time."

Maybe. Maybe it was.

"Have I answered all of your questions? Addressed everything you've been thinking?" He drained his wine glass.

"Yes."

"Do you have any other questions for me?" He took my glass and drank its contents in one long gulp that put my focus on his throat, his lips. The way he licked them.

"No."

"Did my answers help or hurt?"

"Help." I didn't have to think about that.

He tugged my ankle until my back was flat on the couch. His fingers went to the button and zipper of my pants. "Can we do something else now?"

"Please, God."

His laugh was dark. My sigh was soft when his mouth met mine.

∞

Cassidy

"I WAS WONDERING when you would come down," Gran said.

She was right to wonder. The smell of melted beeswax called to me in my sleep and pulled me from my bed. It led me into my kitchen where I made two cups of tea and wrote a note for Cahir, still asleep in my bed. And didn't that make me smile? To know that body with its corded muscles and desire to please laid where I left it. Laid where I drained it after a long night of reaching for him. Riding him. Accepting him. Pushing him. Touching him in places he hadn't been touched before. Making him familiar with the dark. A lover of it.

Gran was in the back of her shop behind the glass that gave everyone full view of her workshop. Sometimes shoppers would abandon their carts to see her pour candles or polish her own crystals. To see her bead jewelry or clothes in the way the Kenyan women taught her. Her hair was covered by a turban. Her face carried a light sheen of sweat. Her hands never wavered as they passed over each of her molds with hot, melted wax.

I stood next to her at the old work table the man I called Uncle Ernest made for her. I ran my fingers over the heart I carved into it with our initials. My father told me Gran was going to kill me when she saw it. That I would be in so much trouble. But Gran ran her fingers over it and asked me for the knife. Then she carved our initials deeper into the wood.

I took the wax from her and jerked my chin at the tea I brought down.

"You remember how?"

I rolled my eyes and bit back my yelp when she pinched my thigh. I accepted the burn for the first bit of focus that it was and fell into the pattern of breaths she taught me. That batch of candles was for tranquility. Calm. Serene. Worry free. That was what the dictionary said tranquility was. Gran taught me that it was a pleased acceptance. It was the pleasure of life as it existed and the lack of desire to concern yourself with what it would be.

Tranquility wasn't always easy for me to find, but I poured the candles, set the wicks, and felt my mind go quiet.

We would wait for them to cool before we carved anything into them.

"So."

I smiled at Gran. "What if I just wanted to see you?"

"Then you would have seen me and gone back to the man in your bed."

"How much did you hear?"

"You mean how much did I feel?"

No. I said what I meant. Not that something like that would matter to Gran. She wanted the thing she valued most: the truth. It was the foundation for everything for her.

"How much did you feel, Gran?"

"How long have you loved him?"

"I'm not ready to say that I do."

"How long has he loved you?"

"I'm not ready to admit he does."

You gave Gran the truth because of the look in her eyes

when she heard it. Because you could feel her pride in you emanate from her body like a wave that crashed over you and warmed you from the inside out.

"What holds you back from something that should only make you better?"

I looked at her. She was such a graceful woman. There was majesty in the wrinkles joy and time gave her, in the direct, doe eyes that were the exact match to mine.

"There's an insecurity in me."

"Let's see it."

"I've never met the woman he loved before me. I've never seen her. I won't even google her. I don't want to know."

"Why?"

"She broke him and he still speaks kindly of her. She hurt him and he won't place any more blame or anger on her than she deserves. She betrayed him. Twice. And he can look me in the eye and tell me that he can't be with her but he still loves her."

"Show me the rest."

Yes. She would know that there was more. "How can I compete with a woman that can do that? How can what he feels for me measure up to that? How can I build something new with him if there's that?"

"The ghost of a woman."

"Yes."

"Is there more?"

No. That was the big secret. The one that pressed on my chest in the mornings before he reached for me and followed me through Beyond. Screamed at me from behind the glass of her office.

"Well, my love. You seem to not want to see things for what they are."

"Gran-"

She held up her hand. "Love is not a confusing thing. It is a big one. So big that it sometimes pushes things like our common sense out of the way."

I laughed.

"You say he doesn't speak ill of those he invited into his life, into his heart. He doesn't give more blame than what's owed and deserved. I say that doesn't say anything about her. That says something about him, about the kind of man he is, about the kind of man that he will be for you. You see?"

Yes, I did.

"Just because he is good doesn't mean that you have to make yourself small or say that you don't measure up. You have a good man. Mind your business and be a good woman."

I laughed again. "Gran!"

"That's all there is. Thinking that you have to be jealous and insecure not because he's disrespecting you, lying to you, stringing you and another woman along but because he's just good and decent is silly, girl. Stop that."

"And do what?"

She got off the bench and went to the candles. "Enjoy yourself."

EIGHTEEN

Cahir

I THOUGHT I fucked it up that night on my couch. I thought maybe I said the thing I wouldn't be able to come back from. The thing that took the patience out of her eyes and the openness from her face. The thing that made her reach for me even when she didn't need my help.

But she was there. Still there. Not the same though. She came back to her bed late one morning smelling like wax and flowers and made me see colors I didn't know existed. She laughed. She talked. She did all the things she did before. And was somehow still different. Still better. While still being Cash.

It made me push. Try harder. Do more. Look for the places she hadn't claimed yet and show them to her, offer them to her, see if she'd want to move in there too. She did. Even when I didn't expect her to.

But what was a stylist supposed to do with more clothes? What was the daughter of real estate moguls supposed to do with buckets of flowers and succulents from the farmer's market? What was the granddaughter of a seasoned entrepreneur supposed to do with dinner dates?

What did I have to give her that she didn't already have?

Racked my brain and came up empty. It was...odd. That had never happened to me with a woman before. Even with Zion, I knew she had more than she needed but would always welcome more. Things. Give her things.

And I didn't delude myself into thinking that if I had nothing Cash would want me. I knew that she didn't find poverty and struggle attractive. Why would she? Why would anyone? But money wasn't enough. Too common. It had to be more. Different.

And then I had my answer.

We had drinks with Junie. I laughed until I cried like I always did when Junie was around. She swung technicolor braids over her shoulders, popped her gum, and told you things about the world you already knew but hadn't considered in quite the same way she did.

And then I took Cash home.

She moved through my apartment with the familiarity only comfort and time could give. Her purse had a place. Her shoes. The clothes she wore that day and the ones she would wear that night until I took them off of her slowly. As a reminder that I didn't want anything separating her skin from mine. Things were better when my skin was on hers.

We made dinner. No music, no talking. That was good too. Better. Silence used to be heavy, threatening. I used to wonder what secrets it held. What thoughts it concealed. With Cash it felt like-Like when my mom did the laundry when I was a kid and I used to bury myself under those warm soft clothes. Comfort. Security. Rightness.

Dinner was quiet. The long looks between us said

enough. The looks changed when I laid the rose quartz keychain with its single key and fob on the table.

"What is that?"

"Rose quartz." I ran a finger over the raw stone. "I soaked it in salt water and charged it like you taught me. In the window during a full moon."

And, shit, I liked the way her body angled towards mine.

"What's on it?"

"What you need to get into the building."

"Why?" Her voice was soft. Timid. Her eyes wide.

"I-" I cleared my throat. "Because I wanted to give you a gift. Something you didn't have. Something that would matter to the both of us."

"So you're giving me your home?"

I looked around the apartment. "I mean, I'm renting it. I don't think it's mine to give."

She laughed the way I hoped she would.

"Access, Cash. To me. Whenever you want. I'm giving you a permanently open door."

"Did you give Z-"

"We don't have to do that you know." The chair pressed hard into my back.

"What?"

"Every time I do something for you, we don't have to take a moment to compare it to what I did for Zion. This is for you."

"Uh-huh."

She was graceful when she stood. When she walked across my apartment and put on her shoes, grabbed her purse and car keys, and left.

I sat at my dining room table like a jackass. For twenty minutes. I couldn't figure out what I'd done wrong. I couldn't make myself call her and find out. I didn't want to know. If I didn't know there was a chance she would just come back.

"You didn't lock the door behind me," Cash said.

She stood in the doorway, an oversized box in her arms.

"Why don't you ever lock your door?"

I laughed, kissed her, sighed in relief, and looked down into the box.

"They're for you," she said.

I carried the box to the counter. She pulled the plants out and distributed them around the apartment. I remembered them. She would take clippings from herbs, plants, flowers from the farmer's market and put them in little clear glass vases with long necks.

They'd grown. Leaves and buds and fragrance filled my space.

"You can see the water," she said. "So you won't have to wonder if they need any."

I nodded.

"I wanted to give you a gift too." She touched my face.

I took off her clothes.

∞

Cahir

A NEW PATTERN. A new twist. She didn't give me a key, but I didn't really want one. It was enough that she would be there when I got home from work. It was enough that she smiled. That she was closer still and her laughter was a bit brighter. It was enough that when she reached for my hand I knew she reached for someone that was more than her friend.

We went to dinner. Sushi. She complained that there was no good sushi in the City, so I rented a limo for the hour long drive to the highest rated sushi restaurant I could find. And I smiled over our sashimi when I remembered all of the things that we did to each other in that hour.

The restaurant was small. Hidden away in a subway station, of all places. The men that worked there were serious. The lighting was high, for their benefit. There was no thought to setting an atmosphere for us. The music was traditional, light, haunting. And our seats were high so we could peer behind the glass that separated us from the chefs and let us watch them craft masterpieces for us, one simple piece at a time.

Cash held my hand when she wasn't eating. She watched those men stretch salmon and tuna and God knew what else over rice and brush it with something that made everything taste more alive and squeezed my hand as if it were some high drama. She smiled at them and accepted every plate as if it were, of course, the best thing that ever happened to her.

The joy on her face...I forgot to eat until she nudged me and whispered that I was being rude.

I held her hand when we left the restaurant and walked through the subway station. She stopped to listen to a woman with an acoustic guitar scat and dug my wallet out of my pocket to give the woman money. I laughed. And I had to tell her.

"I think I would stay with you."

She turned to face me after we stepped onto the escalator. "What?"

"If Zion fixed everything, if she came back to me with not a single issue, I think I would stay with you."

"That's good but," she touched my face, "thinking isn't as good as knowing, Cahir."

∞

Cahir

I TOOK her to Miami for selfish reasons. I was a man that wanted to see his girlfriend in less. I wanted to see her skin bronze in the sun. I wanted to see her hair curl tighter because of salt water. I wanted to lay beside her in the sand and whisper all the things I wanted to do to her until she dragged me to a cabana we didn't pay for or back to the hotel.

I wanted to take salsa lessons with her and eat Cuban food. I wanted to drink tequila and watch other men fall under the spell her beauty cast. I wanted to know what color the sunset would make her eyes.

Girlfriend.

That's what I said she was when I went to the front desk and asked them to send breakfast up to her while I was at the gym. When I called the florist and asked them to have flowers delivered to her at Beyond when we got back from our trip. It was what I said in my head every time I looked at her and it made me smile. I didn't stop smiling. I wanted to know if she would smile too.

"I've been calling you my girlfriend in my head for about a week now," I said when we were settled on the private jet I chartered to take us home.

"Have you?"

I pulled her onto my lap. "I don't know what that face means. I think this is the first time-"

"-I've made an undecipherable face?"

I tickled her ribs. Her laugh was like...

"I've been calling you my girlfriend in my head. With strangers."

The silence that fell over us-even that silence was comfortable. I traced circles over her back. Her arms looped around my neck.

"Call me your girlfriend out loud," she said when we were at cruising altitude, surrounded by blue sky and clouds. "Say it to me. Make it real."

Her lips were soft when she kissed me. They always were. And yet it always felt new.

"You're my girlfriend."

NINETEEN

Cahir

I TOOK her to her apartment because she asked. Because it made sense. I couldn't have her every second of every day. Because our love was different. I was different. I didn't need to be stifled. I didn't need to drown. I kissed her. I carried her luggage to her apartment. I carried the shopping bags that filled my trunk and filled me with pride. My wealth had a purpose beyond myself. I kissed her again. I laid her across her bed and spread her open. Wide open. Legs. Mouth. Arms. Spirit. Mind. And I gorged so I would have a taste of her when I went home.

Home.

I didn't know where home was. I knew what my address was. But when I went there without Cash it didn't feel the same. Sometimes I touched her plants-my plants-and thought of her. Sometimes I looked through the refrigerator full of the foods we purchased and at the recipes suspended by magnets on the door. I opened her wines and had only a glass. Then I remembered what I wanted most was her. The taste of her. Laughter and teasing and serious and playful and sometimes quiet or bored. I wanted those tastes to fill my mouth.

I thought it would be unbearable, but I found it was nice to miss her. Nice to find the pieces of her that went unnoticed when she was there and became precious when she wasn't.

I drove to my address. I had only one bag to bring in. She bought me clothes but said they were for her house. For her closet. So I would have a place there too. Wasn't that what boyfriends and girlfriends did?

It made me smile. I fished my keys out of my pocket and smiled.

The door opened.

I went inside. Ready to answer emails to binge watch the shows I abandoned because Cash didn't like them for one reason or another.

"Welcome home, Cahir."

I didn't think. I just stepped back into the hall and let the door slam shut millimeters from my nose. How had she gotten in?

TWENTY

Cahir

I TOOK A DEEP BREATH. Another. One more. Hand on the knob but, no, I still wasn't ready. My hand shook. Shook. Why? It was just O'Shea.

I knew of the New Money Girls, the original three, before the fourth was added. Two sugar babies and an escort. They fucked the right men and got rich. They flaunted their wealth and their beauty throughout the City and didn't care how the women felt about it. Except for O'Shea. It was whispered that she was the wildest, the one to fear. The other two ignored the women, the wives. O'Shea befriended them. They cried on her shoulders and told her their secrets. They ate weekly at her restaurant. Threw parties, board meetings, fundraisers, their children's weddings and rehearsal dinners there. And they knew. They knew for the right price she would sleep with their husbands right under Domingo's nose.

They loved her in spite of it. Sometimes I wondered if they loved her because of it.

Long locs fell down her back. Gold hoops at her lip and septum declared she didn't give a fuck so there was no point in asking. And there was paint. Paint everywhere since she'd retired from sex work and revealed she was the artist whose work graced most of our walls. If we were lucky enough. Rich enough. Paint everywhere but on the crater of a diamond on her left ring finger that threw light like a supernova.

I heard she was married. I was happy for her. In another world, I would have danced at that wedding. In another world, I would have called her my sister.

And the only reason why she would be sitting on my kitchen counter with a salad in her lap and a perfectly symmetrical sandwich beside her was if that other world was trying to barge its way back in.

I took a deep breath and opened the door. It was quiet when it closed.

"O." I called her the same thing Zion sometimes did when she talked to me about the friend, the sister, she loved most.

And it must have been right. She beamed at me.

Not that it mattered. O'Shea wasn't a woman that needed favors. What she didn't have her husband could afford. Or she could scheme her way into. She was a businesswoman. A good one. But she didn't want to buy anything. She would have gone to my office. No. This was personal. This was about Zion.

I kept my eyes on her. The way I did my cousin Connor's snakes. I found them fascinating. Beautiful. And I knew they would be fascinating and beautiful after they bit me. I threw my keys into their place. Put my bag down. And she watched me. No. More than that. I felt her sizing me up.

Studying me. I decided then that she was not a person I would want to meet in a dark alley.

She crunched on the salad.

Start easy. "Did you make a-Did you make dinner?"

I leaned on the counter she sat on and peered into the bowl. Damn. It actually looked pretty good.

"Of course not. I'm having dinner with Guy later." The hand that wasn't shoveling food into her mouth brushed across a necklace.

I whistled before I could stop myself. I thought I was territorial. I thought I had a problem with marking my territory. How many diamonds were on that necklace? And would Cash let me put a necklace around her neck that said "cherished" in the swirling font exclusive to bamboo nameplate earrings found in the back hallway of the mall?

She laughed. "This is a snack."

I don't know why, maybe it was the same magic she threw over those wives, but her laughter shifted something in me. I took her fork and tasted her salad. It was good. "Some snack."

She looked almost wistful. Then apologetic. "She's back."

No shit. I snorted. "She never left."

Her eyes narrowed. Snakes, I reminded myself, snakes.

"She's pregnant," O'Shea said. "Pregnant, pregnant."

The fork fell out of my hand. It barely made any noise when it hit the ground. Or maybe I just couldn't hear around the ringing in my ears.

I stood there with it. That word. Pregnant. The world shrank to nothing. Absolutely nothing. And I knew I would die in that nothing space. I wanted to. It would be better that way. I didn't want a baby. I didn't want to tell Cash.

Cash.

How in the fuck was I going to tell Cash?

I picked up the fork and got two clean ones. I took small bites of O'Shea's salad. If I was eating, I couldn't vomit, right?

We finished the salad together. Then O'Shea pulled the prettiest Damascus knife I'd ever seen out of a holster around her ankle.

"Don't tell Guy," she said.

"That you have a knife?"

She rolled her eyes. "That I'm using it to cut a sandwich."

I almost asked what else the knife was for then I remembered the rumors that Guy had turned both of Domingo's ankles to dust. I chose to laugh at the absurdity of the situation instead. I took half of the sandwich when she offered it to me and almost died. It was perfect. She turned the charcuterie Cash and I snacked on when we were too lazy to cook and made it something otherworldly. I would crush a man's ankles for her too.

"She never left?" There was sympathy, concern in the words. For me.

Yeah. I would have liked having her as a sister. "Emails. Notes taped to my door or slid under it. Flowers. Foods we liked. In the beginning she would be there. The lobby of my building. Restaurants I was at. I used your name a lot. With the restaurant managers. To get some privacy."

"I know. Why do you think you got the privacy in the first place?"

We laughed. And it was more familiar. Easy.

"I never pressed it." I took our empty dishes and loaded them into the dishwasher. "She never approached me. It was like she just wanted to make sure-"

"-she stayed on your mind."

"Yeah." I ran a hand over my face. "Could have told her I didn't need help with that. And I didn't want to hurt her more than..."

I shrugged. What else was there to say? Was there a good way to explain it?

"She stopped. Maybe four or five months ago. The notes, the appearances. All of it just stopped." I didn't mention the flowers. Those didn't count. The surprise restaurant appearance didn't either.

"She was showing. In a way she couldn't hide."

And I knew. I heard O when she said it. But suddenly it was new and I understood. "She's pregnant?"

"Gotta be due soon. Weeks, max."

Weeks. No. I did the math. Not a few weeks. If it were mine, I had twelve weeks until my child was born. And that wasn't enough time. Not enough time to decide. Not enough time to tell Cash, to make her see that I didn't want to go back, that I wasn't going back.

The same anger that made me put my fist through a mirror rose up in me. If O'Shea weren't there...

"I'm going to make it worse."

O'Shea sat her phone on the counter beside her and there was Zion's voice as she told her sisters that she'd poked holes in the condoms. All of them. That she got pregnant on purpose. Because that was supposed to fix our relationship. That was supposed to tie me to her forever. I heard shattered glass and the word rapist. I heard O'Shea promise Zion that she had better pray she wasn't pregnant because O'Shea would never let her raise a child.

"I'm a woman that keeps my word." O'Shea's eyes were cold. "That means all of our lives are going to change. And it isn't just you. You have to think of her."

Oh, yes. Snakes were fascinating and beautiful and

knew where to strike. I let my face fall into a smooth mask and confusion enter my voice. "Her?"

O'Shea looked proud of me. The way a mother did when her child brought home his ugly drawings. There was patience there. Kindness. "There's too much food in this kitchen. Too much wine. Candles all over. You have bondage tape and condoms in your freezer. Great idea, by the way. Stupendous. So, yes. Her. What will she say?"

It was one thing to have someone break into my home. Another to have them break into my life. And I knew. I knew what Cash would say. I knew how she would react. I knew how her body would move when she left me.

"She's important, right? You love her?"

"Can you-" I almost choked on my voice. My words. "Can you go?"

She put a hand to her middle. It was the second time she did that. And she hopped off my counter. "No problem. It's time for me to go tell my husband I'm pregnant anyways."

I really choked and said the first thing that came to mind. "Life ruiner."

And we laughed. Until she walked out of my front door.

Then I laid my forehead on my counter and cried.

TWENTY-ONE

Cassidy

I NEVER CALLED Kevin my boyfriend. We laughed and we fucked but we never reached that level of intimacy. And then I found out we never could.

There's something about losing even the possibility of a thing that cuts like a bitch. To know that even if you wanted it, and you didn't before, you couldn't have it. It becomes almost an obsession. It chases you through your own mind and taunts you with your lack. Because that's what it is. You aren't even good enough to have the things you don't want.

I took a deep breath before I told Cahir that I was his girlfriend, that yes, it was okay. And still the fear rattled me. There was nowhere to hide. If losing the possibility of a thing was a bitch, what was losing the real thing? What would it feel like to have it snatched from my hands?

But that was worry for no reason. Worry I didn't need to borrow. Because it was Cahir. My Cahir. My friend. The best one. Even if love wasn't enough friendship would carry us through. I knew that. I felt that.

I smiled at him when he left my apartment. Then I didn't hear from him for a week.

On the first day, I remembered that he had a big pitch coming up. I remembered the last pitch and how he locked himself in his office with his team. The fifteen hour work day he pulled. The way he said it was best that way. He could focus on one thing. And he was glad I understood that. So I didn't say anything. I just had dinner delivered.

On the second day, flowers arrived from him with a note about Miami and what we did in the cabana. I blushed and I dug out more lingerie. I went to his house and stretched across his bed. I woke up in that bed alone the next morning.

The third day I called. Even his secretary didn't answer.

On the fourth day, I forgot how to breathe. That was what not having him was like. Forgetting how to do something you never thought to do before. I didn't know where to eat lunch. What to talk about. What to laugh about. I didn't know how to have conversations with clients, with Junie. I didn't know what to eat for dinner or to watch on tv. I didn't know how to sleep.

On the fifth day I dug. And then I dug a little more. I shoved things out of the way and dug deeper still until I found anger. I dragged it up to the surface and wrapped it around me. I cursed myself for a fool.

Because the anger wasn't real. If I felt rejected, the anger would have been real. If I didn't trust him, the anger would have been real. If I thought he would betray me, betray his word, the anger would have been real. But there was none of that. There was only worry.

Was my friend okay?

∞

Cassidy

ON THE SEVENTH day I called Junie and Gran and begged them to come to my apartment. Junie's hair was the exact same pale pink as the bubblegum she popped.

"So what is this? A 'we hate men' session? A general cry? A 'let's just pretend he doesn't exist'?"

I shrugged my shoulders and plopped down on my couch. "I don't know."

"Then I don't know whether to give you Hennessy or water. Help me help you."

"Is there Hennessy in your purse?"

She pulled out a bottle. "And wine in case you wanted to cry. That's glamorous."

"What if I want to forget he exists?"

"Then I'm pouring you a glass of water. Drunk bitches always remember the one thing they shouldn't."

I laughed and laughed.

"Well that's a nice sound."

"Gran." I ran into her arms.

"I brought you food. You sounded stressed. You never eat when you're stressed." She put a plastic bag full of styrofoam containers on the counter.

"Mother's?" Oh, God. Most of it would be better if she brought me food from Mother's, the best soul food restaurant in Strawberry Fields, if not the whole city.

She nodded. And Junie jumped up off the couch to grab a container out of the bag.

"Hey! I'm the one in crisis here. Shouldn't I eat first?"

Junie rolled her eyes at me. "Girl, please."

We sat and ate. Gran and Junie kept the conversation moving. They even made me laugh. And then the food was gone, silence fell, and I knew it was time.

"I haven't heard from Cahir in a week. Not a text. A phone call. A-nothing. I call his office and there's nothing."

"What do you think happened?" Junie piled up our empty containers and threw them away.

"Now why would she speculate about that?" Gran let one eyebrow rise. "Why would she make excuses for someone that doesn't care enough to make them for himself?"

Junie nodded. "That's fair. Okay. Better question. What are you going to do about it?"

"What?" That wasn't what I wanted to talk about. That wasn't something I wanted to consider.

"Auntie May is right," Junie said. "We can't worry about why he did what he did. We can worry about what you're going to do next."

Gran nodded.

"I-" What was I supposed to say? "I don't know."

"Bitch, if that's all you've got to offer, you could have sat by your damn self in the dark." Junie unwrapped another piece of gum. "Try again."

"I want him to tell me why." I felt like I was going to be sick. "I want to know if this is who he is. If he thinks this is okay. And I want him to..."

"Finish," Gran said.

"I want him to give me answers and if he can, I want him to come back. I want him to be mine."

"That's real cute," Junie said. "You should do all of that. Tomorrow."

"Tomorrow?" That soon? Didn't I need time to pick out the right outfit? To rehearse what I would say and what he might say? To visualize the right outcomes?

"I'll drive," Junie said.

When Gran nodded and patted my shoulder, I knew

the decision was made. It didn't matter that I wasn't ready, that I couldn't swallow the fear that in less than twenty-four hours I might lose Cahir forever.

∞

Cahir

I DIED a little bit after O'Shea told me. Every day. Just a little bit more of me broke away. Pieces of the future I imagined for myself, my life with Cassidy. My business. God. I spent hours in my office. I had to know if it was possible. Could I be a father and still be myself? Could I-

I didn't want Zion. Hearing that there was a baby didn't make me want to go to her. It didn't make me pity her. It didn't make me angry with her. It just made me sad. Tired. I couldn't sleep at home with Cash's plants and the sheets that smelled like her. I slept in my office and dreamed of the baby. Always a little girl. Always. My eyes and her mother's grace. A smile that lifted me and made me promise over and over again to protect her and give her the world.

Then the dream changed. My little girl torn out of my hands. Zion's screams. Disappearing again. But with my baby. A hostage. My beautiful little girl was a pawn and a tool. A way to control me. Because that never changed with Zion. It was never about me. Never. The only worry was if she was happy.

I would wake up and the dream would follow me. It didn't matter. I told myself that. It didn't matter if Zion wanted to use a baby against me. I would give her money for the kid. I would tell her that they could both stay away from me. And I would be free to live my goddamned life. I could have Cash.

I walked around with that for a day. I considered it. I could just not tell her. I could pay Zion to keep away. I could have my lawyers draft something. I could get a restraining order. And Cash would never know. I wouldn't lose her. I would be happy. I would make her happy.

But I had the scars on my hands to remind me of what it was like to have the ability to make decisions for yourself taken away. I knew what it was like to have secrets break you. I knew what it was like to realize the person you loved was so selfish they were willing to hurt you if it meant their happiness.

And if she stayed? If Cash stayed once she knew? She wasn't the kind of woman to want a man that ignored his child. She wasn't the kind of woman that would agree that money and a blind eye were the answer.

And so it went. Back and forth. Over and over in my head. I didn't sleep. More caffeine. Coffee in the morning and energy drinks at night. Wrinkled shirts and pants until my assistant took pity on me and went to my apartment to get me clothes.

After a week of that, I called myself an idiot and went home. I showered. I changed the water for my plants. I stopped at my favorite coffee shop and got an Americano. I stepped into my office at 7:45 in the morning and felt almost like myself. And then I saw O'Shea sitting behind my desk.

It made sense. Cash's voicemails and texts weren't the only ones I was ignoring. In fact, I should have expected her sooner. I walked to my desk and sat in one of the chairs that faced O'Shea and waited.

She grinned. "If you don't ask question, I can't give you dramatic answers. Come on, Cahir. Play with me."

I almost smiled back at her. Almost. "How'd Guy take the news?"

She brushed one hand over her stomach. Another over her necklace. "He already knew. Loser. But after dinner he took me to the Club and showed me what he could do with a knife and wax."

I winced. "Little sister, why do you think I wanted to know that? Lie to me. Hide things from me."

"Could I be?" She leaned forward. "Your sister, I mean. I've always wanted an older brother to annoy."

"I would have been if-It would have been fun. I thought that after you left. It would have been fun to have you as a sister. You would have been my favorite."

"Yes, I would have. Fine is my favorite. But he helped me rob a place once so I don't think you should be jealous. But you could be. Jealous, I mean. It would be perfectly understandable."

No. It wouldn't be. But like every other conversation I had with O'Shea, it was perfectly absurd. No matter how serious it was supposed to be. I tilted my head back and laughed. I laughed until I cried. Until I had to put my coffee and phone on the desk so I didn't drop them.

"What else should I ask you?" I dried my eyes.

"The obvious."

She was having so much fun and I didn't want to talk about the other thing. "How did you get in here?"

"Well." She let the silence between us build. I imagined her kicking her legs under the desk. "When you really get down to it, the problem with capitalist societies is that a small group of people hold all the resources and the wealth and once you know a few of them-"

"Toots's husband owns the building," I said when I

remembered that O'Shea managed to make friends with every monied woman over the age of sixty in the City.

She stuck her tongue out at me.

"Sorry."

"Yes. I'm sure you are."

I grinned.

"Ask another."

"Why'd you break in?"

"Because," she kicked her feet up on my desk and laughed when I rolled my eyes. "It occurred to me that you were going to keep kicking me out, keep dancing around the real problem, keep avoiding all those lovely voicemails I left you until we addressed the secret."

I should have known. The easy smile I wore dropped off my face.

"Aren't you going to ask which secret?"

Did she think I was an idiot? "No."

"Good. We are on the same page." She took her feet off my desk and propped her elbows on it instead. "You're in love with Cassidy."

I sit back in my seat. Mind fast, words slow. "How did you know?"

And she smiles. Proud I didn't waste her time with lies and denial. "I was there. When you came in for your first styling appointment. I stood in Delia's loft and looked down at you and had the biggest feeling of deja vu I've ever experienced in my life. I couldn't figure out why, where it was coming from. I went back to my studio instead of trying to stand there and figure it out, or making it obvious that I was staring at the two of you like idiots. I realized what it was a bit later. It was the same kind of... You know?" She waved her hands. "It was exactly what happened to me the first time I saw

Guy. The same kind of daze. The same kind of confusion because all of a sudden reality was something different."

Well, that was nice. That she saw it before Cash or I did. That was fun.

"I knew." She grinned. Having fun. "And you came back too much. She went to your office just a few more times than she should have had to. But otherwise you two did a great job keeping it low-key. My sisters don't know."

Relief made my shoulders sag.

"Was that it? You didn't want us to know?" She tilted her head. "That hurts my feelings a little bit."

"You loved her." I didn't have to say Zion's name. The mere allusion to her made something in O'Shea deflate. She looked down at the desk. "You loved her more than I did, and I didn't know how I was going to breathe without her. How was I supposed to tell you that I moved from her to one of Delia's employees? Delia's only employee? What am I doing? Preying on you guys?"

"Oh. Guilt. That's stupid. We're way too logical to blame you for who you fall in love with. And we like you. Remember? We like you a lot."

"I like you guys too."

"But I'm the favorite."

I chuckled. "Yeah, kid. You're the favorite."

"Now that we've established that for the second time-" She clapped her hands together. "To business. You want the baby or what?"

"What if I don't?" I took my first sip of coffee.

The answer didn't matter. Not really. I just needed time. Every time I saw O'Shea it was like I was being clubbed over the head.

"I guess I'm going to be raising two kids. And figuring

out a way to make you want to be involved even if you aren't a primary caregiver."

"You'd do that?"

"I'm pretty sure Guy would agree to it."

"Are you?"

"He's never told me no before, and I ask for some pretty outlandish shit."

"Wow." I laughed. And then the laughter stopped. When would I ever tell Cash no? When would I ever not provide what she needed, what she wanted? "I love her. Cassidy."

"Yes. We've covered that part."

"No. No, we haven't. Not really. I didn't mean to. I fought it like fucking hell. She did too. For the record. She fought it as hard as I did. But when we were done fighting, the feelings were still there and she's-" I threw my hands up.

"Take your time."

So many words. But I wanted the right ones. I wanted to tell the truth about what Cash was for me. What she'd done to me. "She didn't heal me. I did that. She didn't make it possible for me to trust again. I did that. But she gave me what I needed to get to that place. She gave me a reason to get my shit together and my head out of my ass."

"I know that feeling." She wrapped a hand around her necklace.

"I love her so much that for a second my answer about whether or not I wanted a child depended on her, on whether she would stay. But that's not fair. To me or the baby."

"You're going to be a great father."

"Yeah, I am." I pushed all the air out of my lungs. There it was. The truth. And I couldn't look away from it "Fuck. I'm going to be a father."

O'Shea bounded around my desk and hugged me. "You're going to be great. I'll help."

"Will you?" I couldn't keep the amusement off my face or out of my voice.

"Of course. I'll be a huge help. I'll start by talking to Cassidy for you. As an advocate. After you tell her." She grabbed her bag and rushed to the door. A little hurricane.

"O- I don't need your help."

She stopped. Her hand on the door knob. "Of course you need my help. You're a man. And you have no idea what you're going to say to her."

My coffee was cold. My laughter was warm.

TWENTY-TWO

Cahir

"I REHEARSED what I was going to say." Cash's voice was low. So low I thought I'd fallen asleep at my desk and dreamed it up. "I was going to be mean. Accusatory. I wanted a good fight."

She was tired. I saw that. Her make up was flawless as always but I saw the puffiness under her eyes. The way her hand shook when she brushed back her hair. A tremor.

Sadness hit- heavy and unwelcome. Because I did that. I made my friend worry. I ran from the woman I loved and didn't think of what that would do to her. All that talk that I was better and I still ended up in the wrong place and with the guilt of doing the wrong thing.

"I thought," she stepped further into the room. The setting sun made her brown hair an unnatural red. "I thought I would hurl insults. I thought I would puff up my chest and ask you who the fuck you thought I was. I thought I would curse and scream until your shame made you two inches tall and then I would go."

I wanted to hold her. I wanted to feel the heat and flash that flare to life every time my skin came into contact with hers. I wanted to tell her I was so sorry and that there was a simple explanation. But what's simple about a baby with your ex?

So I sat behind my desk, mouth closed, heart pounding.

"What I would like to know is why," she said. And the tremors stopped. She didn't look so weary anymore. "Decide you don't love or want me. Go back on your word. You're a man. I'll find the space to accept it if I can't forgive it. But the silence. The avoidance. We're friends."

Yeah. We were. And I would lose her if I told her. I couldn't-The moment had arrived and in spite of everything that happened to me, in spite of the scars, I couldn't open my mouth.

"Do you know I don't think I'd leave you? Because of the friendship. If you told me why, I would stay."

I couldn't call her a liar. I couldn't let out the panicked laughter that rose up in me. I couldn't move.

"Cahir."

Silence. Dank and thick.

I couldn't.

And then she left.

I sat in the dark with the absence of her and it clawed through me, clawed into me. It was unlike anything I'd ever felt before. And it would be forever if I didn't get the fuck up out of my chair.

Then I heard her words again. All of them. Really heard them.

I took a deep breath and ran out of my office, down the hall to where Cash waited for an elevator.

∞

Cassidy

"CASH."

I heard him when I left the office. I heard his stillness. I heard him when he stood. It was why I didn't cry. He wasn't going to see my tears. I would save them for home. For the place that didn't include him anymore.

I pressed the call button for the elevator and prayed to every goddess I could name that it would hurry. But Cahir's legs were long. My prayer was half answered. The elevator whooshed open. Cahir stepped onto it with me.

"I'm sorry," he said. "I'm sorry."

He kissed me.

I should have slapped him. I should have pushed him away from me. I should have wiped the taste of him from my mouth and remembered my pride was more important than my feelings. But that was a lie and Cahir tasted like home. Before I went back to an empty apartment I deserved to have a taste of home again.

I stepped into his arms.

The weariness fell away. The anxiety. I quieted the voices that told me that I shouldn't, couldn't do this, that the pain would be worse when it was over. A little longer, a little more. I pressed the emergency stop button. The elevator went dark except for one harsh blue light that ringed the ceiling.

It was the right thing, or it meant something to him. His hands didn't hold-they grasped. His mouth insisted. His body was flush with mine and the heat of him enveloped me. He was taking me to hell.

And my God, what a journey. Familiar and smooth. Silken. Enveloping. The tug of hair and the stinging bite of teeth on lower lips. Knees wedged between thighs and pushed high to ride. Hands on belts, zippers, diving below waistbands until there was flesh. Sighs. Moans.

Two fingers pressed inside me. Five fingers wrapped around him. The first orgasm was a wave in a violent ocean that had to be heard to be truly felt. So I screamed. High and long with no care for who might hear or come running. The second. For the second, my panties were ripped away. I dragged him with me into a corner and used the rail to lift myself up high and spread my legs wide.

I thought he would step between my legs. He was heavy with me. Red with wanting me. Instead he fell to his knees and slid his tongue inside me. And oh-It was better than home. Better than pride.

Fingers on my clit. His tongue probed. His face was wet, but he didn't stop. And I couldn't stop when I started to come. I wanted to. I wanted to stretch that moment out. I wanted him on his knees, mouth full of me, to be where I spent forever. What was heaven compared to that.

Then he rose. He kissed me and it tasted like a promise he could keep.

"No," I said.

He slid into me. As always my eyes took a moment to roll to the back of my head.

"Yes. I'm sorry. I can say that. Can you? Can you say what you need to?"

I shook my head. This wasn't about me. Wasn't about my secrets.

"I didn't know how I was going to tell you." His hips were slow when they worked him deeper inside me. "I still don't. But then I realized you didn't yell."

"I didn't want to."

"Why not?"

I shook my head.

"Why did you come?" He pinched my clit. "Why did you want answers? Why didn't you just leave me?"

"No," I said.

"I need you to tell me." Truth made his voice raw. Made his words sting. "Tell me so I can tell you why."

"Asshole."

"Yeah." He moved faster. "I am. And a coward. I shouldn't have done this to you. I shouldn't have made you wonder. But I did. Tell me so I can tell you."

The hand that pinched my clit moved up to roll my nipples. To hold my jaw as he kissed me. To hold me in place when his onslaught began in earnest. And it was perfect. Perfect as summer nights or falling into an easy sleep.

"Please, Cash. I love you."

And the truth of it was that I loved him too. Even if I ran from it the feeling was there, right there. As constant as breathing or blinking. As easy and as difficult as smiling. Loved him so much I trusted him. Knew that whatever took him from me for seven days wasn't enough to hurt me, to break me, to break us. I meant it. I would stay.

"I love you too." I gave him the words and then I gave him my body.

And he abused it. Pushed it. Pushed me until I fell into an orgasm that made my body sag and tears fall from my eyes.

I cried out my love, his name, prayers and supplications to a deity without name until my body was still.

Cahir smoothed down my dress and found my heels. He pulled a handkerchief out of his pocket and wiped between my thighs.

I kissed him while he put himself back together and sighed when I was in his arms again.

"I love you," I said. "Tell me why."

"Tell me you love me again," he said.

I smiled into our kiss. "I love you. Tell me why."

His arms were tight around me. His lips on my fore-head. "Zion is pregnant."

I didn't hear the words right away. No. I heard them. And rejected them. Pregnant? Zion? Cahir? No.

"Cash?"

I looked at him. Blank. I must have looked like an idiot.

"Cash? Say something."

"I ought to bust your face in with a brick."

ALSO BY JIMI GAILLARD-JEFFERSON

The New Money Girls

The New Money Girls

Zion, Nadia, Delia, and O'Shea have lives, dreams, and rich men who love them — but sex and money aren't always everything! Four friends will become a sisterhood in this sizzling page-turner.

Never Too Much

Sex and money aren't everything but that doesn't mean Zion, Nadia, Delia, and O'Shea can't have both. It doesn't mean they can't have it all. But can they be satisfied with having all of their dreams come true? Is happily ever enough?

Talk that Talk

Delia, O'Shea, and Nadia find out what happens to women bold enough to have it all and face consequences that will change them, and their sisterhood, forever.

Going to Hell

They were friends that became sisters and business partners. To keep love, ambition, their business, and their lifestyle, they'll have to become so much more.

Control

In the final book of the New Money Girls series, O'Shea, Nadia, and Delia will be tested in ways they never imagined. It's a good thing they have each other...

Guy

He saw her and knew. O'Shea saw him and resisted. He's never backed down from a fight- especially when his heart's on the line.

A FREE Standalone Novel.

The New Money Girls Complete Box Set

All five novels in the New Money Girls series in one place!

Tony and LeAndra

Belong to Me

Will king pin Tony quit the game for love? Will wealthy LeAndra give up her world to become a part of his? When their worlds collide sparks fly but so do tempers.

Conquer with Me

There's blood on her hands and at his feet. Can Tony and LeAndra rebuild their lives and the love they once shared?

Rule with Me

Can two lost souls find their way back to love and live life the way they'd planned: happily together?

Tony and LeAndra: The Complete Series Box Set

All three novels in the Tony and LeAndra series in one place!

Cassidy and Cahir

Better as Friends

He's strictly off limits. His ex ruined his life. Before he can move on I have to be sure his past is truly behind him.

Better than Your Ex

She lost him. She thinks it's over. She doesn't know that he's coming for her, that she's the love of his life.

Better as Lovers

He agreed to give her time. She agreed to stay by his side. Can the couple who had a bright future ahead of them, find their way past the obstacles and build a better future together or is it too late?

Friends to Lovers: The Complete Cassidy and Cahir Series

All three novels in the Cassidy and Cahir series in one place!

CPSIA information can be obtained
at www.ICGtesting.com
Printed in the USA
LVHW092037061120
670968LV00007B/1103